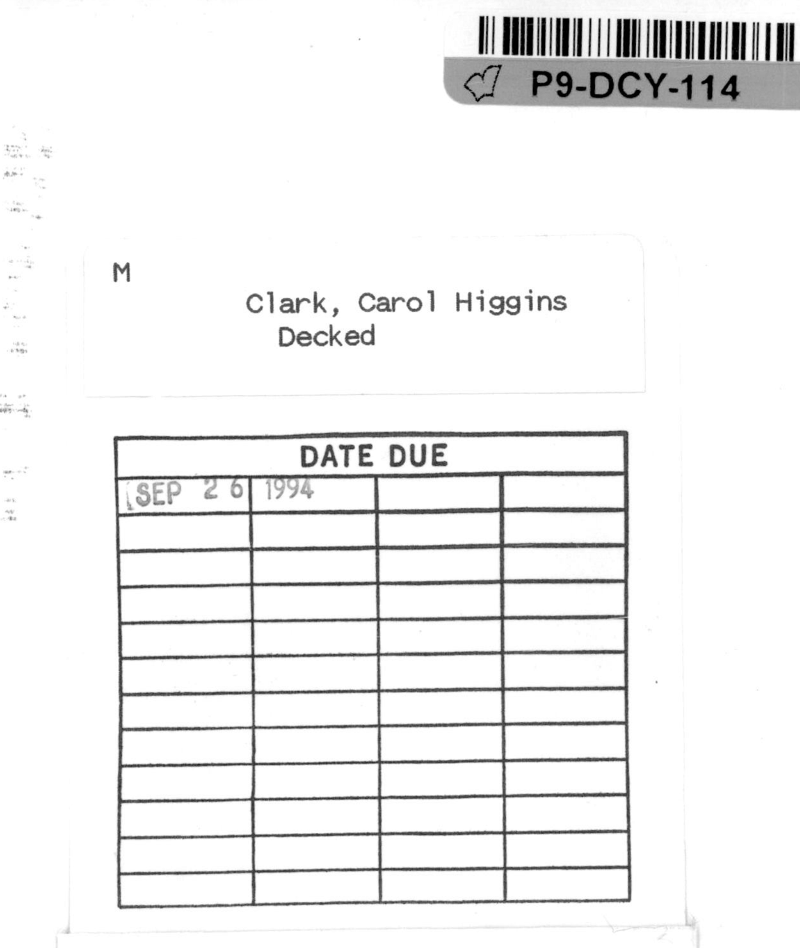
M
Clark, Carol Higgins
Decked
DATE DUE
SEP 26 1994

DECKED

DECKED

A Regan Reilly Mystery

CAROL
HIGGINS CLARK

A Time Warner Company

Warner Books, Inc., 1271 Avenue of the Americas, New York, NY 10020
A Time Warner Company

Printed in the United States of America

ISBN 0-446-51549-3

For my mother, Mary Higgins Clark,
and in the memory of my father,
Warren F. Clark,

With love.

"Old and young we are all on our last cruise."

—Robert Louis Stevenson

DECKED

Prologue

Friday, April 23, 1982
Oxford, England

ATHENA RAN BLINDLY down the dark country lane, her breath coming in short, harsh gasps. Her school jacket with the St. Polycarp's logo sewn on the pocket was no protection against the sudden drenching spring rain. The knapsack strapped to her body impeded her flight. It did not occur to her to discard it.

As the bewildering shock began to wear off, she desperately told herself she was a fool to have come this way. The Oxford police station was so much nearer. Minutes ago she would have reached safety there.

The wet, uneven road was becoming more visible. Trees heavily burdened with thick dripping leaves were no longer silhouettes but three-dimensional objects that beckoned to her.

A car was coming from behind. Athena shrank to the side, instinctively sensing that she must not be seen.

Headlights froze on her. The car raced forward, crunched to a stop inches from her feet. The door opened.

Her fingers fumbled to release the knapsack as she started to run again. Sobs caught in her throat. She heard the footsteps gaining on her.

No—no. Just turned twenty-one, she was finally free to live on her own. She couldn't die now. Her fresh burst of speed granted her another hundred yards before hands found her throat.

Friday, June 19, 1992
At Sea

GAVIN GRAY HURRIED down the hallway, crashing into one handrail and then the other as he struggled to keep his balance. "If I weren't on a ship, I'd think I was drunk," he mumbled. But he didn't care. His adrenaline was pumping so much he felt light-headed. Another reason to bounce off the walls.

The ocean liner he was sailing on, a magnificent floating city, had hit rocky seas tonight. It would be another day and a half before they docked in Southampton, England. Not soon enough, he thought as he lunged his way to the safety of his cabin. He couldn't wait to see land again, and the weather they'd experienced during this crossing had nothing to do with it.

He had already spent enough time on this mammoth vessel playing host to a bunch of old broads. "Let them find someone else to make an idiot out of himself doing the cha-cha. No more black and blue marks for me," he cackled under his breath.

On these long transatlantic crossings, there was always an abundance of unescorted females. Hoping to help even the odds, the cruise line had hired him as a sixty-two-year-old host—a roving companion who would be only too willing to whisk them off onto the dance floor and suffer the brutality of their aimless kicks.

Just this morning he had been teaching the polka to an enthusiastic octogenarian wearing black bulky shoes. They were like gunboats hinged on her thick ankles, targeted for his luckless feet. Gavin winced when he thought of it. Stomping on someone's foot was supposed to be a form of self-defense, not a recreational activity.

Reaching his cabin door, he slipped his key into the polished brass keyhole and sighed in grateful relief. He sat down on his bed, lay back, and stared up at the ceiling as he tried to catch his breath. Funny how these cabins are so much smaller than the way they appear in the brochures, Gavin thought. Really funny for the poor slobs shelling out thousands to park their behinds on these bunks for a dreamy week at sea. Victims of trick photography.

He turned and looked at the digital clock next to his bed. Eleven thirty-two P.M. Should he go to the casino and get a nightcap? Be seen? Charm any of the single ladies still awake? He certainly could use a brandy to calm his nerves. No, he finally decided, he had better not. Most people had retired to their rooms early tonight, the stormy seas, not Mr. Sandman, being the reason.

"No, I'll just stay here," he whispered to himself. He had had enough excitement for one night.

He couldn't believe his luck. Just as he was heading out of the Lancelot Bar he'd run into old Mrs. Watkins. Sweet unassuming Beatrice Watkins with her splashy jewels and liquored breath.

For days, she'd made no secret of the fact that she was very alone in the palatial Camelot Suite. There was no need for trick photography when capturing the essence of that little home-away-from-home. It boasted a living room, a sunken bedroom, two baths and a private terrace which afforded an exclusive view of the sea and sky that one could enjoy at any hour of the day or night. Christ, anybody could get laid with that setup. Gavin wondered if Mrs. Watkins had gotten lucky yet. She flirted unabashedly with everyone. Slipping the busboys her room number wrapped in hundred-dollar bills. Plying the hosts with champagne as if it were water. Even the Captain wasn't immune.

Tonight at the Captain's party she had hobbled over to have her picture taken with him four times. She was bedizened with all her finest jewelry. An antique diamond-and-ruby tiara resting precariously on her bony skull; six rings on her fingers, each with a larger stone than the next; matching diamond-and-emerald wrist and ankle bracelets, the latter wrapped around her bird leg.

The Captain was as charming as ever. He tilted his silver head down toward her matching one and smiled merrily for the camera. He thanked her and moved her along, graciously greeting the next couple of happy cruisers. He even pretended not to notice as she teetered off, grabbed another glass of champagne from a passing waiter, gulped it down and unsteadily got in line to have her picture taken again.

How does the Captain do it? Gavin wondered. That professional smile frozen onto his face as he had his picture taken hundreds of times, two consecutive nights out of a five-day cruise. Two Captain's parties to accommodate twelve hundred passengers. Twelve hundred sets of teeth, a majority of them held in place by Polygrip, had to hold the "cheese" position before Captain, my Captain, could escape. He must wake up with a smile, Gavin thought, and for all the wrong reasons.

After dinner and a few more drinks, Mrs. Watkins decided her old bod deserved a much-needed respite from one of the favored activities on cruise ships all over the world, drinking to excess. Perfecting the art of intoxication. She was stumbling past when Gavin saw her and offered to help her back to her suite. She hiccuped her assent and gladly grabbed his arm as the catch on her bracelet snagged his jacket.

"Oh, I have to have this thing fixsht. Otherwise I'll looge it," she fussed.

Gavin only smiled at the prospect.

Mrs. Watkins's eyes grew heavy as Gavin helped her stagger to her penthouse. I've got some job, he thought wistfully, jackassing people around a ship. But always the gentleman, he helped her with her key and guided her inside. She flopped down on her bed, fell back and immediately passed out. But not before the bracelet slipped off her wrist.

He had stood there staring, not wanting to move. Not knowing what to do. Suddenly, visions of financial independence danced in his head.

Who wouldn't believe it had fallen off at some point during the evening? She had been babbling that the catch wasn't working. People saw how wasted she was. She could have dropped it anywhere.

Could he risk taking it now? What if they started a search for it? The cruise line loved this woman. She always paid a pretty penny for this suite and would often book it on a whim. If anything made her unhappy, they immediately did their best to fix it. No, he'd have to hide it here in her suite and then, when the excitement of losing it had died down, he'd make his way back in and get it. Somehow.

Giddy with excitement, his armpits sweating, his heart pounding, he tried to figure out what to do. Her Highness was sprawled across the king-sized bed. Three steps up to the right was a loftlike living room complete with pastel couches, a big-screen television, state-of-the-art stereo system and a bar. A sliding glass door to the balcony lined one wall. And then his eyes caught it. The closet with the life preservers. They had already had their boat drill on this cruise, so there'd be no reason for anyone to go in there again . . .

He tiptoed over to the bed. Holding his breath, he leaned over to pick up the dazzling assemblage of emeralds and diamonds. Fenced, this thing must be worth a million bucks, he thought incredulously. A tantalizing thought bubbled through his brain. Maybe I should just help myself to her other little goodies. He entertained the thought for a moment as he caressed the bracelet. As usual, his Irish-Catholic guilt overwhelmed him and prevented him from committing a real no-no in the mortal-sin category. To his mind, stealing one bracelet from someone this rich should only count as venial.

Mrs. Watkins stirred and mumbled something about the Captain.

I'd better get out of here, Gavin fretted. Some jerk might have seen me steering her back. Better just to take the bracelet than get tempted by other thoughts. After all, once he had a few bucks he might meet a beautiful younger woman with plenty of her own jewelry who would want him. He was smart enough to know that it would have to happen soon though, and it would only happen if he had a little money to throw around. His looks were fading fast. Some might say they had already taken a hike. His hair was graying more each day and his muscles were beginning to sag out of control. He had gotten the shock of his life when he had gone to a movie recently and had been offered the senior citizen's discount. An offer he almost foolishly refused.

Shaking that ugly thought from his head, Gavin clutched the beloved trinket in his well-manicured hands and crept over to the closet. He slowly unlatched the door and cringed as a whiny creaking sound announced his arrival to the orange life preservers staring down at him from the shelf, mocking him, as if to say, "You'll never get away with this." His nerves screaming, he stood on his tiptoes like an aging ballerina and tossed the bracelet behind them to the distant corner of the high shelf.

"I shall return," he murmured.

Like a cat he sprang across the room, blew a loving kiss at Beatrice Watkins, and slithered out the door.

The crew would be turning the ship upside down looking for that bracelet. But when the ship docked Sunday, they'd stop looking. They'd be sure someone had found it and, like any red-blooded thief, had kept it. He'd try to sneak up here and get the bracelet in the hours of the layover. But if he couldn't manage that, on the trip back to New York he'd find a way to visit this suite and retrieve it.

Nothing was going to stop him from getting that bracelet back.

Saturday, June 20, 1992
Oxford, England

REGAN REILLY WOKE up slowly, blinked eyes that felt glued shut, and looked around trying to figure out where the hell she was. Forcing the fog from her brain she scanned the dormitory room before registering that the white-blond hair sticking out from the skimpy covers on the narrow bed across from her belonged to her best friend Kit.

With a sigh, Regan lay back down, turned on her side, and watched the gray light filter through the small window in the corner. She and Kit had arrived the night before to celebrate the tenth reunion of their Junior Year Program at St. Polycarp's in Oxford. And they were just in time to greet another dreary day in England. I hope it cheers up by this afternoon, Regan thought as she pulled the paper-thin blanket around her clammy skin. A lot has changed but the weather certainly hasn't. It's what Athena hated most about this place.

Athena. It was disconcerting to think about her. It's hard to believe that I shared this very room with her, Regan thought. Until she took off to go to London for the weekend at the end of April ten years ago and never came back. And no one had heard from her by the time the term ended in June.

Athena hadn't been the easiest person to live with, always complaining and wishing she were back in Greece. Getting into her bathrobe after her 10 A.M. English class on Mondays, Wednesdays, and Fridays, and staying in the room all day. Blowing her nose constantly and never allowing Regan to open the tiny window for a breath of fresh air. Refusing Regan's early offers to join the crowd for a beer down at the local pub. So when Athena turned twenty-one and inherited money from her grandmother, Regan hadn't been surprised that she never came back from her weekend jaunt. "I've learned enough Eeenglesh," she was always telling Regan, "no matter what my parents say."

Well, it's for sure she won't want to come back for this reunion even if she does hear about it, Regan thought. I almost didn't come myself.

It was Kit who had urged Regan to make the trip. "Look, I know you're free. For God's sake, you're written up in last week's issue of *People* for solving your big case. I think we should go to Europe and celebrate. Take a couple of weeks off. It will be fun to see the old gang again."

Originally Regan had planned on going to law school, but sometime during her senior year of college she had finally opted for investigative work. After graduation she had taken a job working for an older detective in Los Angeles who had taken her under his wing. A couple of years ago she had finally struck out on her own. But her career choice worried her parents, Luke and Nora Reilly.

Her father, a funeral director, protested that her good looks couldn't help but attract "the wrong kind of people." Her mother, a well-known writer of suspense novels, took full responsibility, adding, "It was all those trials I took you to. I never should have done it." Regan had reasoned with them, "I have a father who owns three funeral homes and a mother who spins yarns about serial killers. And you want me to get a 'normal' job?" To their continuing dismay, Regan loved her work.

That last job had been to trace a father who disappeared with his two young children. As she told her parents, witnessing the reunion between the mother and the little boys was worth all the endless hours of following dead-end leads.

She and Kit had begun their vacation in Venice, then met Regan's parents in Paris. Nora was just winding up a publicity tour for her latest novel. "If anyone asks me again where I get ideas for my books, I'll kill myself," Nora had sighed. Then she'd asked Regan penetrating questions about the kidnapping. Nora and Luke were sailing Monday on the *Queen Guinevere* to New York. Nora might enjoy a few days in a deck chair, but Regan knew her mother's mind would be spinning out a new plot, and it probably would involve custody battles.

Now, as Regan studied the contents of the room, bits and pieces of memories slowly began to surface in her mind. Well, they certainly haven't wasted any money on an interior decorator in these ten years, she mused. The threadbare grayish-green carpeting, the ancient nondescript wallpaper, the "temporary" closets that gave new meaning to the word, the little white scratched sink with a foggy-looking mirror hanging above, the dormers you had to be careful not to hit your head on when you got up in the morning, and finally the two pieces of lumpy foam on wheels that were passed off as beds. Ah, the price you pay to be a part of history, Regan thought. To have studied in Oxford . . . Although St. Polycarp's wasn't actually a part of Oxford University, if you said you had studied in Oxford, people were impressed. They should see these rooms, Regan thought.

The covers rustled on the other bed. Regan looked across the room and laughed. Kit had pulled the blankets over her head and was clawing the top of them, the only visible part of her anatomy being her fingernails.

"Nice try, but they have to be black," Regan laughed.

Athena's slumbering position had been famous in the dorm. They had teased her that her long black fingernails sticking straight out when she was sleeping made her look as if she was either about to attack someone or was frozen in an advanced stage of rigor mortis. The sight of them had taken Regan by surprise more than once when she returned home after a night of partying.

Kit relaxed her hands and opened her eyes. "This bed. My back is broken," she moaned.

"What, the accommodations are not to your liking?" Regan asked in disbelief as she stretched and got up. "If you really want to get depressed, think about the food we used to eat here, Slop à la Saint Polycarp's." She gathered up her soap, moisturizer, shampoo, cream rinse, loofah and towel in her arms and started for the door. "Another thing I don't miss is carrying this stuff in a bucket to the shower. There was something so industrial about it. Made me feel as if I was a cleaning lady with a mission and my body was the first room of a dirty house. See you."

When Regan returned, wrapped in a terry-cloth robe, she alerted Kit that the coast was clear.

"Nobody else seems to be around. But if you have a Janitor in a Drum in your Samsonite, invite him to shower with you."

Kit groaned. "Oh, it can't be as bad as it was."

"Worse," Regan laughed. "The drain is so slow that the water backs up fast and your feet get a good slimy soak. We should set up a booth for pedicures and a fungus dip outside the bathroom."

Regan dressed quickly, pulling on jeans, sneakers and a yellow cotton crew-neck sweater that had been given to her by a former boyfriend only after his maid had shrunk it in the wash.

Approaching the fog-strewn mirror, she plugged in her travelling hair dryer and bent over. Crunching her dark permed hair, she remembered the hours she had spent at this sink drying her waist-length parted-in-the-middle tresses, and silently prayed that none of her former classmates had brought along old pictures.

But it was the same pair of blue eyes that stared back at her when she straightened up and looked in the mirror. The only time they looked different was when she used colored contacts in an attempt to avoid being recognized on a job. And she thought thankfully, her size-eight jeans still fit.

She reached for her cosmetic kit. As she opened it, the smell of White Linen wafted across the room. A purse-size vial of the perfume had spilled all over everything in her pocketbook, including her English money. She laid some still-damp bills on the dresser. The now older-looking face of Queen Elizabeth stared up at her reproachfully.

"Sorry, Your Majesty. But it does smell good."

The door of the bedroom opened and was slammed shut with a vicious bang. "I slipped on the moss in the shower," Kit snapped. "And I scraped my butt on the drainpipe. I wonder if Jacoby and Meyers has a London office."

Jacoby & Meyers was the New York law firm whose television commercials urged you to sue your grandmother if you tripped over her hand-crocheted rug. Kit's sun-streaked hair was still wet from the shower. Water was squishing from her five-and-dime thongs. Her travelling robe covered all five feet three of her slender frame.

"A plumbing salesman would starve to death in these parts," Kit continued. "And to think Thomas Crapper was an Englishman. They should pay more homage to his memory."

"I feel responsible," Regan said humbly. "I should have told you to wear shoes with cleats. Anyhow, let's get out of here and go downtown."

EVEN FOR ENGLAND, it was chilly for mid-June. The sun was trying unsuccessfully to cut through the clouds. Regan and Kit, both dying for a cup of hot English tea, quickened their pace as they hurried into town to the Nosebag. Regan poked Kit as they passed Keble College, famous for its ugly exterior in the midst of so much architectural beauty.

"Remember having dinner there? That was incredible. It was so regal seeing all those guys in their flowing black gowns and watching the faculty parade into that ancient dining hall with the long wooden tables."

"All I remember is Simon correcting me on which spoon to use."

"Oh yeah."

At the Nosebag, a cozy restaurant known not only for its Laura Ashley decor and good food, but also for its soft classical background music that was unobtrusive but just loud enough to create an atmosphere, they found four of their classmates who had also come back for the reunion. They immediately merged to a larger pine table, ordered, and over a full English breakfast began the inevitable "Do you remember?" From there they progressed to "Have you heard? . . ." The hot news offered by Kristen Libbey, who had arrived three days early and had had a chance to catch up on the gossip, was that Professor Philip Whitcomb was finally getting married.

Regan lead the incredulous wave of "You have to be kidding!"

"Well, after all," Kit said thoughtfully. "He is only in his early forties. He's not bad-looking . . ."

"What?" Regan interrupted. "He's wimpy-looking."

Kit ignored her. "He really is a good teacher." They all nodded in agreement.

Regan interjected. "He always seemed like the typical perennial bachelor. All his time off he spent gardening at his aunt's place. Who is he marrying anyway?"

"A teacher who came the term after we were all here," Kristen told her.

"Did they just discover each other, or have they been planting daisies together for the past ten years? What's her name anyway?" Regan asked.

"Val Twyler. Rumor has it she's been after him for the past couple of years. She teaches English Lit, is a few years younger than Philip, very intellectual and very efficient."

"Well, she'd need to be to be married to Philip," Regan added. "He never wore matching socks or tucked his shirt in properly. Oh my God, look who's coming!"

They all turned to see Claire James push through the line full of people waiting for tables. Obviously she had spotted them. Ten years had not changed her preference for L.L. Bean outfits with matching headbands.

"Hi, y'all," she drawled. "How come nobody came to git me this morning? I just never sleep this doggone late."

It was obvious, Regan thought, that Claire was still playing the Southern belle.

Claire looked around. "You guys all just look super. And Regan, I just love your new little hairdo. You look so much better with it short."

Under the table Kit stepped on Regan's foot with significant pressure. Regan refilled her cup of tea as Claire, obviously assuming they'd all be fascinated to hear, filled them in on the fact that she had been married, divorced, and was now engaged again. "And I've travelled and travelled," she concluded airily. "Regan, I always pack one of your mother's books to read on the plane.

Where does she get those crazy ideas? That last one had me so skay-ud. Did you know I looked up Athena's family in Greece last year?"

"Is Athena back in the family fold?" Regan asked.

"No, she is not. They never heard another word from her. Wouldn't you think she'd at least send a postcard?"

"She never showed up!" Regan exclaimed. "And they never tried to trace her?"

"After a while they tried. But she just vanished into thin air."

"I wish I had known," Regan said. "Nobody just vanishes into thin air."

Claire dismissed the subject with a wave of her hand. "Did any of you read the reunion schedule?" she continued. "Before the dinner tonight, Philip's aunt, that sweet dear old lady, has invited us for cocktails at her house. Remember she gave us a farewell party ten years ago?"

Regan remembered. She remembered the drafty old house, the muddy grounds which even then Philip was miraculously turning into an English garden, the Cheez Whiz on a stale biscuit, and, best or worst of all, Philip's aunt, Lady Veronica Whitcomb Exner.

At age forty, half her lifetime ago, to the total astonishment of her relatives and friends, Veronica had married Sir Gilbert Exner, then eighty-six years old. He quite considerately died of a heart attack two weeks later, leaving much speculation as to whether Veronica's untried libido had been set free in the drafty master bedroom of Llewellyn Hall.

Regan was rather fond of Lady Exner. But then again she had only seen her in small doses. Ten years ago Veronica Exner's sole social activity had seemed to consist of having her nephew the Professor invite his students over for sherry. Regan realized Claire was still talking.

"I think they're goin' to announce Philip's engagement tonight," Claire declared.

"I haven't seen Philip since we left this town," Kit reflected.

Regan realized she hadn't seen Philip since that last night when they got into a discussion about Athena. She remembered now that Philip's assessment of the situation had turned her off, yet in an odd way had been a comfort.

"It's one of the hazards of being an heiress," he had said. "In a year or two she'll have run through her inheritance and be back home with Daddy. Wait and see."

Regan found herself wondering whether Philip knew that Athena had never gone home to Daddy.

After breakfast they spilled out onto the Cornmarket, where legendary traffic congestion, throngs of people, and the addition of three fast food chains belied the fact that by just stepping behind the college walls that lined Oxford's downtown area, you could be transported into another world where medieval charm remained intact. Tradition and progress were always at odds with each other in this picturesque town of soaring spires, exquisite gardens, flowing rivers and wide open spaces. Known as the "cyclist's city," it was also a major manufacturer of automobiles.

After wandering around for no more than half an hour, the group decided to split up. Everyone had a different agenda and it was too hard to keep track of each other in the midst of all the Saturday shoppers.

"Let's rent bicycles and ride around the countryside," Regan suggested to Kit.

"I sure could use the exercise. Let's do it. They probably have the same bicycles we rented ten years ago," Kit replied.

"Oh God, I hope not. I don't feel like spending the afternoon trying to put the chain back on mine," Regan said, remembering her bicycle's knack of falling apart on deserted roads three miles out of town.

They rode around Oxford, commenting with disgust on all the new construction. They swung down to the southern part of town, cycled past Christ Church Meadow, and at one o'clock they stopped for lunch in a pub along the Cherwell River. They sat at a table by the window and breathed in the scents of the damp earth that was slowly being warmed by the tentative sunlight, and the musty, oaky smell of the pub. It brought back memories of the Keble boys with whom they had gone pub crawling.

"God only knows what happened to those guys," Regan pondered as she took a sip of rust-colored lager. "Wouldn't it be fun to see them again?"

"Oh, they're probably all working in London and making piles of money," Kit replied as she looked out at a relaxed group punting slowly down the river.

"It's hard to believe that when we knew them they were the future leaders of this country. Remember knocking on Ian's door?"

"If it's a boy, I'm getting dressed. If it's a girl, come on in," Kit said as she imitated Ian's lyrical Welsh accent. "I wonder what he would say now if he saw you pull out your gun and snap handcuffs on somebody."

"He'd probably ask to borrow them."

Over a meal of shepherd's pie they expressed surprise at Claire's ability to snare another guy when she didn't seem to have any redeeming qualities.

"But Kit, we've never met either one of them. I can just imagine what they're like."

"Like your blind date who wore the big furry hat into Spago's?"

"Exactly. And to think he was listed in some magazine as one of the ten most eligible bachelors in the country."

"You never told me that. What magazine?" Kit asked eagerly.

"I don't remember the name," Regan replied, "but I think his mother was the publisher."

At four o'clock they returned to the dorm, observed for themselves the invitation to Llewellyn Hall, decided they could squeeze in an hour's nap and in their room dove again for the cots with the dank green bedspreads.

Two school vans, whose new-car smells had faded away sometime in the late sixties, were waiting at 6 p.m. to pick up the fifteen alumnae who had shown up for the reunion and take them for the two-mile drive to Lady Exner's house. As the van bounced along, Regan began to catch up with some of her former classmates she had not yet seen. On one level her mind was registering how some people looked different, others almost exactly the same, while absorbing what they had been doing over the past decade. On another level her mind was insistently serving a nagging worry that had begun this morning when she'd learned that Athena had never resurfaced.

The driver of the van, one of the new young professors, almost overshot Llewellyn Hall, slammed on the brakes and went into immediate reverse, throwing them all back and forth like kernels bursting into popcorn. "So sorry," he chirped more to himself than the others as he steered the van down the long oak-lined driveway, rattling to a stop in front of the mansion.

Kit turned to Regan. "Are we having a good time yet?"

Faint moans of agony accompanied the movements of the visiting alumnae as, stooping and bending, they stumbled out of the van on their insulted limbs.

"I need a drink," Regan heard someone mutter.

I need two drinks, Regan thought.

Lady Exner had obviously been watching for them. The great entrance door of Llewellyn Hall flew open and with crows of delight she started jumping up and down with glee, rattling off their names as though she'd seen them yesterday.

"Oh my God, look at her." Kit sounded awestruck.

The last time they had seen Lady Exner, her iron-gray hair had been pulled back into a fierce bun, and a pleated wool skirt, high-neck long-sleeved blouse with a silver brooch at the neck, inset with her mother-in-law's picture, and Scottish wool sweater had been her de-rigueur manner of dressing. Now she had on an iridescent gold silk suit with a matching cowl-neck blouse that swooped low on her chest.

From directly behind her Regan heard Claire observe, "I swear she must go to your hairdresser, Regan." Regan resisted the urge to trip her even while she acknowledged to herself that Lady Exner's militant bun had been transformed into a crinkle-cut perm colored the same as the gold suit.

Lady Exner was not reluctant to talk about the metamorphosis as she escorted them to the drawing room overlooking the garden. "I had a heart attack four years ago," she said almost gleefully. "The doctor warned me, 'The heart is getting tired and you need to be careful.' You know what I told him? I told him I've been careful all my life except for my two-week odyssey with Sir Gilbert. I went straight home and made a list of all the things I wished I'd done in this lifetime but had been afraid to try. And now I'm doing them all!"

She fluttered her gnarled blue-veined hands and wrists. "See these rings and bracelets? I always loved my friend Maeve's jewelry. I never had any jewelry except for the pin with Sir Gilbert's mother's picture on it and her wedding ring. When Maeve passed on to a higher plane last year, I decided, why not? The estate had to sell her jewelry to raise money for the taxes, and now it's mine, all mine. Lovely, isn't it? I bought new clothes, changed my hairdo and, best of all, I'm taking trips. Philip insisted I have a companion. Here she is."

They were at the entrance to the drawing room. This, Lady Exner had clearly not changed. Victorian sofas in fading damask, an Oriental carpet whose colors were virtually indistinguishable, horsehair chairs by the fireplace, portraits of long-forgotten Exners all of whom looked as if they suffered from the heartbreak of psoriasis, and a tea table burdened with Lady Exner's usual cocktail offerings: anchovies on damp-looking toast points, a bowl of limp potato chips and a mound of fish pâté that suspiciously resembled bird droppings.

A rotund woman whom Regan guessed to be about sixty, with short-cropped hair, large round glasses and an anxious expression, was studying the serving table. A fiftyish wiry bean pole in a maid's uniform was at her side.

"Everything looks perfect," the woman declared, the anxious expression clearing from her face. She turned, smiling. "Ah, Lady Exner, we're just ready for your guests."

A moment later Regan's hand was being crushed by the vigorous grasping squeeze of Penelope Atwater. "Your mother's books have made our travels so pleasant. Lady Exner always buys two copies hardcover. We read them at the same time, and whoever figures out the murderer buys the other one the first sherry of the day. We'd both love to meet Nora Regan Reilly and discuss her plots with her, and where she gets her ideas, and—"

"Ten years ago I told Regan her mother should write my life story. Now it's that much more interesting. I've been gathering my notes and journals," Veronica said gaily.

Regan, knowing that Lady Exner had written to her mother a couple of times with ideas on how they could novelize her memoirs, decided to ignore the hint. "Tell me about your trips," she said.

The two women beamed at each other. "Well, we started by going to Spain," Lady Exner told her. "That was four years ago. It was wonderful. I met so many nice people. They say the English are reserved, but not me." Her hearty laugh revealed that she had also invested in new dentures.

"The only trouble was that I get so much agida from all the spicy food," Penelope told her with a mournful sigh.

"And we went to Venice last September for the blessing of the fleet," Veronica continued. "All my life I wanted to see Venice, and I wasn't disappointed."

"The scungilli they served in Saint Mark's Piazza really set it off," Penelope informed them.

"Set off what?" Kit asked as she joined the conversation.

"My agida," Penelope replied forcefully.

Regan got the impression that Penelope Atwater's agida was a constant topic of conversation during their travels.

"Well, let's hope your stomach holds out on the *Queen Guinevere* next week," Lady Exner said. "Once that ship pulls out of Southampton, that's it for you for the next five days."

"The *Queen Guinevere*?" Regan tried to keep the dismay out of her voice. "You're sailing next week?"

"On Monday. I've always wanted to go to New York, and my cousin's daughter has been writing to me so much these last few years. I never met her but she seems like such a dear girl. Only forty years old, has had three marriages to men who took advantage of her sweet nature, and is now struggling to raise two daughters alone. She wants us to stay with her and get to know them. And then I hope I can persuade her to come here for dear Philip's wedding in September and maybe even stay for the year. Her daughters could go to school at Saint Polycarp's and they all could live with me. Who knows? They might want to stay forever. We have so little family as it is."

Veronica's plans for her newfound cousins did not interest Regan. What terrified her was that Luke and Nora would be on that crossing.

It was obvious Kit had the same thought. "Regan, isn't that the ship your moth—"

Regan gave Kit a warning pinch as she broke in, "We're all so anxious to see Philip again and meet his fiancée."

"Val makes me nervous," Penelope said. "She gives me agida."

"Oh, she's quite all right," Veronica said. "A bit overbearing, of course, but Philip needs looking after, and I won't be here forever. Now I really must see some of the other guests."

The maid, wearing an expression that seemed to signify permanent resignation, was passing a tray of sherry. Regan and Kit each plucked a glass and escaped to stand by the window.

"I'm sorry I almost let the cat out of the bag," Kit told her. "But I suppose it wouldn't have made much difference. She's sure to hear your mother's on board, and once she knows it she'll never give her a minute's peace."

"Not necessarily. Unless she's on a publicity tour, my mother travels as Mrs. Luke J. Reilly. She tries to avoid the celebrity bit when she and my father are on vacation."

"That's good. Your mother's so nice, she'd have a hard time telling Veronica to get lost," Kit said. "Those gardens really are beautiful, aren't they?"

As far as the eye could see, the property had been cultivated into an exquisite English garden with formal beds of a variety of flowers including old pinks, marigolds, forget-me-nots, delphiniums, pansies and Brampton stocks, all separated by pebble footpaths. Toward the side of the house, a large tract of land had been turned into a vegetable garden.

"I wonder how Philip could possibly have done all that by himself. I've killed so many plants with too much water, not enough water, too little sun, too much sun, no plant food, the wrong plant food. I can't keep a weed alive in my apartment."

"Oh, Regan, I'm just sure you don't give yourself enough credit," Claire trilled in Regan's ear.

Regan had the immediate thought that Claire had all the makings of a private investigator. An ability to turn up where she wasn't wanted and hear what wasn't intended for her ears.

"I'll bet you talk to your plants, Claire," Regan said sweetly.

"You bet. I just chatter away to them," Claire agreed. "Wouldn't you just think that with the way Philip has made these grounds so beautiful, the old lady would spring for a little interior decorating? I mean, there's old, and then there's *old*. Well, maybe when Philip gets married, his wife will take this place in hand."

"It really isn't hers to take in hand," Regan observed.

"Oh, well, you know what I mean. Philip practically lives

here now, and it will be his house someday. And it is a regular oasis with all the new construction in town. I wonder if he plans to turn the whole five hundred acres into gardens. Oh, look, here he is now, and that must be his intended."

There was a surge to greet the newcomers. Veronica cried triumphantly, "There you are, my dear boy. We're all waiting for you to make your announcement."

Philip's blush covered his face and ran up into his thinning sandy hair. "Oh dear, it s-s-sounds as if you already have."

Regan remembered that Philip had a slight stammer when he became flustered. There was no sign of nervousness in the woman at his side. Regan's immediate impression of Val Twyler was that she had a beige look: sandy hair almost the same color as Philip's, a sallow complexion and pale brown eyes. Her features were sharp, her body taut and angular. She was wearing a tan gabardine skirt, a white long-sleeved blouse and low-heeled brown shoes. Her smile as she returned Veronica's greeting revealed large strong teeth that gave a horsey look to her narrow face, but when Regan was introduced to her, Val Twyler seemed genuinely warm.

"Philip and Veronica have introduced me to all your mother's books. I've enjoyed them."

Philip hugged Regan and Kit. "Saint Polycarp's hasn't been the same since you two passed through here."

They congratulated him on his engagement.

"Don't quite know what kind of husband material I am," he said, laughing nervously, "but Val's a dear."

The maid began moving through the room carrying a tray with the canapés. Her best customer was Penelope Atwater.

"No wonder she gets heartburn," Regan observed to Kit. "She's gobbling up those repulsive hors d'oeuvres smeared with that vile-looking pâté. Well, maybe if she eats them all, they won't notice that nobody else is going back for seconds."

The vans were picking them up at eight o'clock to take them back to St. Polycarp's for dinner. At ten of eight they began to say good-bye to their hosts. The phone rang as Regan was bidding bon voyage to the seafaring travellers, praying that they would not somehow learn that her mother was on board.

The maid summoned Philip. "I asked if you couldn't ring back in a few minutes, but they said it's very important."

A moment later, when Philip returned to the drawing room, his face was drained of color. He said, "I'm afraid there's been a pr-pr-problem. The police superintendent is on his way over. He must speak to all of you."

At the chorus of questions, Philip said quietly, "You were all in her class, you see." Perspiration gathered on his forehead. Regan saw Val slip her hand into his and pat his arm.

"They seem to have found what's left of her body." He gestured vaguely toward the rear of Veronica's estate. "On that building site; it adjoins our northeast end. They were bl-bl-blasting a few hours ago. A watchman noticed something and summoned the po-po-police."

"Noticed what?" Regan demanded.

"Remnants of a Saint Polycarp's jacket . . . the bo-bo-body . . . under some leaves . . . a knap-knap-knapsack with her student card . . ."

"Athena?" Regan asked as a stab of pain wrenched her chest.

"Yes, yes, that's it." His stammer had disappeared. "It does seem as though the body is that of Athena Popolous."

Sunday, June 21, 1992
Oxford

NIGEL LIVINGSTON HAD been the superintendent of police in Oxford for eight years. He had not been there when Athena Popolous disappeared. After her body was found Saturday afternoon and he had had his first meeting with her classmates at Llewellyn Hall, he studied the file carefully. A second meeting was scheduled at Lady Exner's home for the next morning, and Livingston had made notes on what questions he wanted to ask and to whom he intended to direct them.

The sun was shining brightly as he pulled into the driveway of the estate. It had been generous of Lady Exner to suggest that all the questioning be done in her home, he conceded as he got out from behind the wheel of his car, grunting slightly with the effort. He'd put on two stone in the last five years, and now that he'd turned fifty was becoming aware that he had to get into better shape. When he looked in the mirror he was seeing his father's face. A ruddy complexion, lined forehead and heavyset jaw topped with a reasonably full head of salt-and-pepper hair.

He closed the door of his car and for a moment stood silently, appreciating the restful quiet of the lovely property. Hard to believe that property this valuable hadn't been swallowed up in the building boom. It wasn't as though Llewellyn Hall was qualified as an official historic site.

He walked toward the door and concentrated again on the business at hand. As he rang the bell he thought of the people he had met last night and most wanted to talk to today. Topping the list was Regan Reilly, who had been the roommate of Athena Popolous and was now a private investigator. And then there was Philip Whitcomb. That girl Claire had confided to him that she always thought Athena had a crush on Philip, and that ten years ago Philip had been good-looking in a dreamy, poetic way.

The maid admitted him to the house. "They're in the drawing room, sir."

It was evident to Livingston that the initial shock had worn off and the assembled young women had probably talked half the night about the death. A number of them were holding teacups and there was a platter of the hors d'oeuvres he had refused when he came to the house last evening. They looked as though they had been left out all night.

Philip Whitcomb was standing at the window looking out at his formal country gardens, as though the sight of them was somehow giving him comfort. His fiancée, Val Twyler, was standing beside him, her arm slipped through his. Nigel realized that that was exactly the way they had been standing last night, and he had the incongruous thought that maybe they hadn't budged since then.

Lady Exner rushed into the room behind him. This morning she was wearing a bright pink jumpsuit that would, Livingston decided, have been more appropriate for his fifteen-year-old daughter.

"Dear Inspector," she cried, "how noble of you to not take these sweet young girls down to that dreary station. I do hope you won't need to question Penelope much. She was really most distressed with agida last night. However, brave soul that she is, she will join us shortly."

Livingston reflected that since Penelope Atwater had not set foot in Oxford until Lady Exner hired her as a companion four years ago, he would not have been distressed to have her distress keep her out of the way. Last night she had exhibited a macabre interest in the crime and even gone so far as to ask if she could view the body. "Reading suspense has always been my passion," she had told him with a nervous, braying laugh.

Murmuring what he hoped were appropriate expressions

of sympathy, Livingston walked over to the fireplace. All eyes focused on him expectantly.

"The autopsy is complete," he announced. "Athena Popolous did indeed die of strangulation. There is absolutely no question of accidental death. If you'll remember, last night I asked you to try to think of anything Athena might have told you, in however casual a fashion, that might make you think she was planning to meet someone or if she perhaps was quietly dating someone who lived or worked in the vicinity."

As he had expected, the response was generally negative. He tried another tack. "Let's talk about her family again. What did she say about them?"

Again, what he heard was the same as last night. Athena and her wealthy, prominent parents did not get along. On a couple of occasions Athena had told Regan Reilly about her aunt's murder the summer before she came to St. Polycarp's, but then never wanted to talk about it again. Apparently her aunt had left the beach, gone back to her house for her prescription sunglasses and stumbled onto a burglary in progress, a crime that turned deadly.

Athena had hated St. Polycarp's, avoided friendships, and no one was that surprised when she disappeared, particularly since she had just come into a large trust fund from her grandmother.

"Well, I think there was one person who was surprised." Claire's voice was honey sweet. "I know you all don't agree with me, but Southern girls can tell this kind of thing. Athena had a mad crush on Philip. I used to watch her face when he read that sexy Greek poetry."

Philip's face turned scarlet. "Sh-sh-surely you-you-you can't be serious."

Val's eyes and lips narrowed, her face flushed. "That's nonsense," she snapped.

"Now, Val honey, you weren't even here at the time. I didn't say Philip had a crush on Athena. That really would be ridiculous. I said Athena had a crush on him. I just kept thinking about it all night long. After all, the Inspectah did ask us to think on poor Athena."

Kit and Regan were seated on the scratchy love seat.

"I can't believe what I just heard," Kit whispered to Regan.

Instinctively Livingston looked to Regan for her response. "Miss Reilly, you were Athena's roommate. Do you think she had a crush on the Professor?"

Regan thought that Claire had had a crush on Philip ten years ago. Was this her way of causing trouble? "I can honestly say that if she did, I didn't notice it. But you must understand, it was impossible to get close to Athena. I gave up trying."

Livingston's arm had been on the mantel. He straightened up. "Well, if anything comes to mind that any of you think might be helpful, please let me know."

"Terribly sorry. I'm so dreadfully late." Penelope Atwater, her face pale and shiny with perspiration, made a somewhat bedraggled entrance into the room. The pockets of her oversized wool cardigan were jammed with crumpled tissues, the tops of which peeked out in unlovely disarray. Her gathered and rumpled skirt reached unevenly to the general area of her mid-calf. Her flesh-color lisle hose lay in exhausted folds around her ankles, kissing the top of her Reeboks.

"I must find out where she shops," Kit whispered to Regan.

"Val, you're a love. That pot of tea really settled my nasty little tummy."

"Little tummy?" Regan whispered back to Kit.

Like a homing pigeon Penelope swooped on the tray of hors d'oeuvres. "Can you believe I'm actually hungry? A few hours ago I never wanted to see food again. As they say, you've got to get right back on the horse . . ."

"Never mind getting back on the horse, we have to get on that ship tomorrow."

Regan thought that Veronica's voice had a slight edge to it. She didn't blame her. She knew Veronica had her heart set on this trip and needed the rather dubious companionship of Penelope.

Awed, she watched Penelope shovel a stack of hors d'oeuvres on a cocktail napkin which she arranged as a carrying case.

Livingston's voice was filled with weary resignation as he said, "You really should not have troubled yourself, Miss Atwater. And now I do want to apologize to all of you for having to take up so much of your time during your brief stay in Oxford." He turned to Philip. "You have no plans to travel, I assume, Professor?"

Philip's face turned scarlet again. "Absolutely not."

Again Val's face registered indignation. "Philip and I are in charge of the summer program at Saint Polycarp's. We'll be staying here to look after the place while Lady Exner is away. You can reach him at any time."

"Quite so," Livingston replied, his voice offhand as he turned his gaze on Regan. "Miss Reilly, you of all people had the most opportunity to hear something that may have seemed insignificant. I realize it's been a long time, but your mind is trained for investigative detail . . ."

Regan joined him at the fireplace as others refilled their teacups. "I've been trying to remember anything that might help. I kept a journal while I was here that's packed away at my parents' house in New Jersey, along with pictures I took. My parents are away now, but when they get back next week, I'll ask my mother to send it to me in Los Angeles. I have a feeling it might trigger something." She smiled at Livingston. "At the time I thought it would be crazy not to try and capture on paper my impressions of Oxford." Her smile disappeared and she looked thoughtful. "Of course I never thought I'd end up searching it for clues in a murder investigation. But I did live with Athena for eight months, and her name appears in it many times. There might be something . . ." Regan turned as Val offered her another cup of tea. "No, thanks, Val."

"I appreciate your help," Livingston said as he bowed slightly.

"I'm scheduled to leave tomorrow, but I'd like to remain in

contact with you and do anything I can to find out who could have done this to Athena."

"Absolutely."

Regan suddenly felt as if the room seemed too close. It was almost as though the smell of death were in it. She realized that the scent of flowers coming through the open windows was reminding her of the Reilly funeral homes. She turned to Kit. "Why don't we walk back?"

"Good idea. We can stop at the pub down the road," Kit whispered.

Hurriedly they again extended good wishes to Philip and Val. "I'll be thinking of you on your big day," Regan said, "September fourteenth, isn't it?" She shook Penelope's hand and kissed Lady Exner's rouged cheek. "I know you'll love sailing to New York," she said.

"I'll keep careful notes of my journey," Veronica promised, "so that when I finally get to meet your mother I shall have a complete account of this new adventure in my remarkable life. You must give me your mother's number. I understand New Jersey isn't far from where my nieces live in Long Island."

"Your nieces? I thought they were your cousins?" Regan asked.

"Nieces, cousins, whatever."

"Well," Regan said tentatively, "maybe you could get together with my mother for lunch in New York City."

"SPLENDID!" Veronica cried. "Penelope," she shouted, "get me a pen."

For the rest of the day Regan and Kit attempted to pick up the schedule of the disrupted reunion. In the late afternoon they went punting on the river, followed by a buffet dinner in the home of the headmaster.

"A nice spread," Kit commented to Regan. "What do you bet we get letters next week asking for alumnae donations?"

"You're a born cynic," Regan said in a low voice as she

helped herself to potato salad. "We'll just have to pretend they got lost in the mail."

A number of the professors at the dinner had known Athena and invariably the conversation centered on the discovery of the body and the questioning by Superintendent Livingston.

It was 11 P.M. when Regan and Kit finally walked up the two flights to their room.

"I can't wait to get out of here," Kit said. "This dorm seems even more depressing than usual. At least we had a good time in Venice and Paris last week. What time did you say your flight is?"

"One o'clock. Just an hour after yours."

Kit was flying to New York, Regan to Los Angeles.

They were at the room. Regan pulled the key out of her pocket and pushed open the door. There was an envelope on the floor addressed to her. "Call me no matter what time you get in. Desperately important." It was signed Philip Whitcomb.

KNOWING JOLLY WELL it was useless, Philip Whitcomb had tried to dissuade his Aunt Veronica from traveling alone on the *Queen Guinevere*. He, Val, the doctor and a most determined Lady Exner were in the small waiting area down the hall from Penelope's room at Royal Oxford Hospital. Penelope's moans could be heard the length of the corridor. She would be here at least two days recovering from acute food poisoning, and under no circumstances would she be well enough to go on holiday, at least not till the end of the week.

"I am absolutely not going to defer my trip," Lady Exner said vehemently. "I don't care if there is a sailing in two weeks. I may not be alive in two weeks. Penelope can fly over to New York when she recovers. I am leaving tomorrow." Her face took on the mulish look that Philip knew only too well.

"Lady Exner, if I may suggest," the doctor began.

"You may not suggest that I stay home," she snapped at him. "A trip deferred is a trip denied. He who hesitates is lost. Today is the first day of the rest of your life, and tomorrow is the first day of my holiday." Her smile was more forceful than pleasant.

"Don't you think Miss Atwater will feel bad if you leave without her?" the doctor suggested timidly.

"Not nearly as bad as I'll feel if I'm not on that ship. And besides, I told her to stop stuffing her face yesterday." She got up. "I must go home and complete my packing. Penelope is really quite all right, isn't she, Doctor?"

"She's most uncomfortable, really quite ill, but I believe she will be fine," the doctor agreed.

"Thank you. Philip, Val, come along."

"May I make a suggestion, Lady Exner?" Val asked.

"It depends on what it is."

"Not that you stay home," Val said soothingly. "But you'll enjoy the trip that much more if you have a companion."

"Val, who-who-who could you possibly expect to get on such short notice?" Philip asked impatiently. "The bloody ship sails in thirteen hours."

Val's narrow smile was triumphant. "Someone who is already packed, who, according to her own words, has just completed an assignment, and who would probably welcome the chance to spend some time with dear Veronica—Regan Reilly."

Regan listened with increasing dismay as Philip pleaded with her to accept the assignment of playing guardian angel to Veronica for five days and nights.

"If-if-if she goes on that ship alone, I kn-n-now she'll end up in the middle of the Atlantic. A second sherry goes directly to her head, and I'm told the main activity on those ships is drinking. Penelope loves to eat. She could chew her way through an oak tree faster than a hoard of beavers, so-so-so she keeps Veronica's drinking down by steering her to the buffet table instead of the bar. I'll p-p-pay you double your daily rate. It's a twenty-four-hour-a-day job. In fairness, I must warn you. Her sleeping habits can be odd. Sometimes she loves to stay up half the night, which means she will take a three-hour afternoon nap.

"If she naps in the afternoon, at least you'll have some time for yourself," Philip continued.

Double pay, Regan thought. And five days at sea on a luxury vessel. She had the time. She had even called Livingston and offered to stay on for a bit, but he had said that at this point there was really nothing she could do. Maybe when Veronica was napping she'd be able to sneak in some visits with her parents.

"All right, Philip, what time will they pick me up?"

* * *

"You're doing what?" Kit's voice was almost a shriek when Regan explained the phone call. "Reilly, I've got to tell you. I think you've really lost it this time."

"I'm being paid. It eases the pain." Regan kicked off her shoes. "Believe it or not, I'm riding all the way to Southampton in a Saint Polycarp's van with shake-em-up Edwin at the wheel. I'd better get some sleep."

Kit, who had already changed, yawned as she got into bed. "Well, one thing I do agree with. Veronica shouldn't be let out without a leash. But better you than me. I'll drive down from Connecticut and be your welcoming committee when your ship comes in. Hopefully you won't have to be carried off."

Monday, June 22, 1992
London

NOT FOR THE first time in their thirty-five years of marriage did Nora Regan Reilly wish that somewhere along the way Luke had learned to pick up the pace of his speech. That thought was followed by the acknowledgment that she had fallen in love on their first date with his Jimmy Stewart looks and vocal pattern. She eyed him affectionately and then anxiously glanced at her watch. They had been just about to follow the bellman out of their suite in London's Stafford Hotel when the phone rang.

It was Herbert Kelly, director of the Summit branch of the Reilly Funeral Homes of New Jersey, and he had a problem. The ninety-year-old widow of the ninety-eight-year-old former mayor was insisting that her husband be laid out in the central parlor. Unfortunately it had been a bad week for retired politicians in Summit, and the main parlor would be occupied for the next day and a half by a former congressman.

Usually Kelly would have taken care of this matter without bothering Luke, but this was truly a delicate situation. Mrs. Shea was the recognized matriarch of the awesomely large Shea clan and had been Luke's first important client when he bought the then struggling mortuary the year he and Nora were married. That was when, as Mrs. Shea put it, her octogenarian mother had been "gathered by God."

"The other funeral parlor in town doesn't make people look nice and natural," she had told Luke, and had given him the chance to "make Mother look as pretty and content as she was when she watched the 'Ed Sullivan' show every Sunday night. She always looked forward to it."

Luke knew she had also checked out his big parking lot out back. He had worked hard on his first big client. It paid off. The deceased looked as though Topo Gigio had just performed an encore. Since then, the Reilly Funeral Home of Summit had been handling the "arrangements" for members of the Shea dynasty, most of whom lived to a truly great old age. A few had even lasted long enough to see snapshots of their withered visages flashed on television by Willard Scott of the "Today" show.

Tersely for him, Luke had explained the problem to Nora to stop her from pacing back and forth in front of him.

The normal solution would be simply to combine the two medium-sized viewing rooms, which were separated by a sliding door. As Nora knew, Mrs. Shea would consider that a second-best solution.

"Tell her the next Shea funeral is on the house," Nora hissed. "Luke, we're going to miss the boat."

Luke's glance was reproachful, and as usual he came up with a solution. "Herbert, remind Mrs. Shea that Dennis's favorite color was green and we've just redecorated those two rooms in green. He'll rest more comfortably there. After all, green and white were his campaign colors."

"You're a frigging genius," Nora said as Luke hung up the phone. "Another problem solved at Reilly's Remains."

"Bad enough I have to hear that kind of talk from our daughter, it's positively obscene to hear it from her mother's lips."

They grinned at each other.

At five feet four, Nora often felt dwarfed by her husband, who was a foot taller. "You're a bigger person than I am in every way," she was fond of telling him. "You don't lie about your age . . ." Luke was sixty-five to her fifty-eight. She could never keep track of what age she had told interviewers she was. "But Mrs. Reilly," one of them had said recently, "three years ago you told me you were fifty-two." And Nora's hair color was a dishonest blond. Luke's silver was natural.

"Now can we please get out of here?" she begged.

The phone rang again. "I don't care if they're looking for a room for the Pope, we've got to get out of here."

Luke reached for the phone, but Nora beat him to it.

"Hello," she said impatiently. "Regan honey, nothing's wrong, is it? . . . I can't talk now. We'll have to call you from the ship. You what? . . . Why? . . . What? . . . Good God . . . I never thought I'd deny my own child, but I guess it's never too late to start. Got to run. See you there, love." She hung up quickly.

"See her where?" Luke demanded. "What was that all about?"

Nora began to laugh. "You'll never believe it. I'll tell you in the car."

Southampton

THE PASSENGER CHECK-IN for the *Queen Guinevere* was located in the vast waiting room between the boat train and the dock. Cameron Hardwick had been told the ship was booked to near capacity and wondered if he'd missed the old lady in a disorganized crowd of twelve hundred people trying to find the appropriate desk for registration. The areas were broken down by class of passenger and then alphabetically. He had been one of the early check-ins at the first-class desk, then sat on a nearby bench, ostensibly deep in the morning paper, as fellow passengers milled around, chatted, complained, and introduced themselves as they waited for the boarding announcement. One and all seemed to be laden down with totes, carry-on cases, and shopping bags with Harrod's name emblazoned in gold.

The first boarding call sounded and the crowd began to surge toward the dock. The lines at the check-in desk thinned. Was the old lady going to miss the ship? The request came over the loudspeaker for all remaining passengers to board immediately.

And then he saw her. There was no missing her. The old girl looked as though she had a sailor's uniform on. White pants, a dark blue top loaded with brass buttons and anchor emblems, and a striped blue-and-white overseas cap. For her age she could certainly move fast. She rushed up to the first-class desk like a runner crossing the finish line.

"Smashing. Smashing," she cried. "We made it. The van broke down three times on M5. Created a most dreadful traffic jam. All those rude people honking and honking." Her voice echoed through the cavernous room, almost drowning out the

Scottish bagpipers who had just struck up their noisy welcome on the dock.

"My expected guest, Miss Penelope Atwater, is presently in a wretched state." She waved vaguely to her midsection. "Tummy problems, don't you see?"

He was aware that everyone in the general area as well as the clerk attending to Lady Exner had the same dumbfounded expression.

"Miss Regan Reilly will share the voyage with me. It's quite all right. Her passport is in order. She'll be along directly. There are quite a few carry-on bags. I have tons of presents for my dear little nieces whom I've never met."

The clerk finally managed to interrupt the torrent. "Your name, madame?"

"Oh, dear me. Of course. Exner. Lady Exner. Veronica. Perhaps you've heard of my husband. Sir Gilbert Exner. He died forty years ago. He was an unpublished poet."

The last stragglers were hurrying to board the ship. Hardwick did not want to be seen staring at Lady Exner. He would have to wait to get a look at the companion. Just as he turned away, he heard Lady Exner's ringing order.

"There you are, Regan. Step smartly. We mustn't miss the boat."

He glanced back over his shoulder and managed to get a good look at Lady Exner's new companion. From behind the mound of packages he could see that she was young and pretty. As he reached for his boarding card he realized that his immediate instinct was that she was also very sharp. This would not be easy.

In the background he could still hear Lady Exner. She was thanking someone for driving her in. ". . . I do hope you get home without further difficulty, Edwin. There's a little tea left in the thermos on the back seat . . . oh dear, Regan tells me I drank it."

There was just one couple ahead of him at the first-class entry. A tall, lanky man with silver hair and a small blond woman. The ship's photographer was about to take their picture. Hardwick cursed under his breath. He did not want his picture taken, but it might look conspicuous to refuse it. He would insist on keeping on his dark glasses.

When the photographer snapped the picture he turned his head to the side. He tried to sound genial when the photographer said, "Let's take another one."

"No. Really. One's enough."

He walked up the ramp and stepped onto the ship. Members of the staff had formed a receiving line to greet the boarding passengers. Piano music was playing in the background. He hung around near the top of the ramp until he saw Lady Exner posing excitedly for the photographer, her arm draped around her young companion, a sea of packages at their feet. The couple he had followed up the ramp were standing near him. The woman was laughing. "It should be an interesting trip, Luke."

You bet it will be, Hardwick thought grimly.

At Sea

THE CAMELOT SUITE was one of two ultra-deluxe penthouses at the top of the ship. Lady Exner fluttered around admiring the pale blue motif as Regan began unpacking. Her own two suitcases she set aside, electing instead to take on the awesome task of organizing the wildly eclectic contents of Veronica's luggage.

She decided that Veronica must have emptied every closet in Llewellyn Hall into the numerous Gucci bags. One oversized valise she opened and closed immediately. It smelled of mothballs and was filled with heavy woolen garments, tweed walking suits, fur-lined boots, woolen gloves and a black velvet cape. "Veronica, are you sure we're not on the World Cruise?"

Veronica was examining one of the closets. "Regan, if we should hit an iceberg just as the *Titanic* did, we must rush directly here for our life preservers. Do you think we should try them on now? . . . What did you ask? . . . Oh dear . . . that's one of the bags I lent Penelope. Philip must have gathered it up by mistake."

Regan felt relieved.

"My woollies are in a different case. I thought we could leave some winter clothes at my niece's for future visits, and of course I'm always worried about a cold snap. But never mind about unpacking now. You haven't even gone out on our private deck. We're about to set sail. Let's go wave to the poor dear people on the dock who won't be accompanying us."

At this point Regan wondered if it wouldn't be so bad to be one of those poor dear people. Luxurious as the suite was, she had been surprised to see that it was really one large open room with two levels. And one king-sized bed. Just inside the cabin door there was a small foyer with a bath to the left. Directly ahead was the bedroom, with another bath off it. Three steps up to the right was the sitting room with sliding doors that opened onto a private terrace. The huge windows offered a breathtaking view of the Atlantic.

I want my own bed, Regan thought. I want to be able to roll over ten times a night without worrying about being mistaken for Sir Gilbert. Polite sleeping for the next five nights sounded exhausting. Veronica was sweet, but sharing a bed was just too much. Regan prayed that the couch was a Bernadette Castro special.

She followed Veronica out onto the deck, which was the highest point of the ship and stretched almost completely to the bow. The front end looked over the roof of the bridge. Veronica pointed to it. "That's where the Captain and all those handsome officers guide us into the wild blue yonder."

The deep boom of the ship's whistle signaled the beginning of the voyage. Veronica rushed to the railing of the balcony and began to wave her overseas cap vigorously in the direction of the dock. The Scottish bagpipers, in one final burst of energy, whined a tinny version of "Sailing, Sailing, Over the Bounty Main."

Veronica sniffed the air appreciatively. "Aren't the sea breezes invigorating?"

"There is something magical about setting sail, Veronica," Regan agreed as she breathed in the salty air. "And now I just want to get the rest of the unpacking out of the way."

"And I shall just stand here and watch the merriment below." From their perch they could lean over the railing and observe the promenade deck two floors down where excited voyagers were still waving and shouting to their friends and relatives.

"Well, don't lean over too far," Regan warned as she started back inside.

"Do pop that lovely bottle of champagne the Captain sent us," Veronica ordered. "We must toast our journey."

Regan thought this might be the best idea Veronica had had since she decided to marry a wealthy knight who had only taken up two weeks of her time.

Veronica quaffed down the bubbly contents of her glass before Regan could even pour her own. She extended it for a refill. "Now for our toast."

Regan remembered that Philip had warned her that Veronica could not tolerate much alcohol. But, she reasoned, she could hardly refuse, and she was safe enough here. She filled both glasses and dutifully clicked hers with Veronica's, who sang, "Bon voyage, dear Regan, bon voyage."

As Regan took her first sip the bubbles tickled her nose. "Good stuff, Veronica."

"It goes down like water, my dear."

Regan prudently carried the bottle back inside. She was taking no chances on leaving it with Veronica. And she wanted to keep busy. The sight of all the happy people saying good-bye to their loved ones suddenly made her feel sad. What were Athena's parents doing right now, knowing that their daughter was never coming home? She tried to push the thought away as she filled the dresser drawers.

I've got to make the best of this, she told herself. It is Veronica's vacation. Next week I'll go over every line of my journal. Maybe I'll find something that will help Livingston.

That led her to wondering whether Jeff was back in Los Angeles. When she left he'd been on location in Canada shooting a mini-series. Regan had initially hired him to help out in her office and go along with her on surveillances when he was between acting jobs. "You're getting too famous for me," she had told him recently. "I can't take you along because people recognize you." But he was always available to bounce ideas off, and he'd been a real help in cracking some of her cases. "Detective work is just like acting," he had said, "you've got to figure out the character's motivation."

She had just jammed the last suitcase in the overhead closet when she heard Veronica shriek, "Monica, Monica, I say, is that you?" Regan whirled around to see Veronica's body bent horseshoe-shaped over the railing. She raced outside as shouts of "Be careful!" chorused from the promenade deck. She locked her arms around Veronica's dangling thighs and yanked her back.

"My God, Veronica, what are you doing?"

Veronica seemed oblivious to the danger. "That woman in the pink hat isn't Monica after all. But what a startling resemblance."

"If you'd leaned over any more, that hat would have been squashed into a beanie." Regan sighed. "Please, Veronica, you must be careful."

"Is everything quite all right up there?" someone shouted.

"Lovely. Just lovely," Veronica yelled down to the dozens of distant staring faces. She gave Regan a glassy-eyed smile. "I hope the rest of the champagne is still nicely chilled, my dear."

Cameron Hardwick had checked to see which dining room they had chosen and was gravely satisfied to learn they were at a table for ten in the King Arthur, the largest of the first-class restaurants. It solved the problem of getting close to them without seeming overt. He had been assigned to a nonsmoking table and had asked to be switched to the smoking section.

Together with the maître d', he studied the seating chart. Trying to seem casual, he pointed to the community table directly at the window on the starboard side. There were eight names listed, including Lady Exner's. "That table looks as though it has a great view. Any chance you could put me there?"

The maître d', a suave, slender man with a seemingly perpetual smile, was delighted to accommodate him. Already working on his tip, no doubt, Cameron thought. It always gave him pleasure to stiff the help whenever possible. Now he would make it his business to get into the dining room directly behind the old bat and Regan Reilly and make sure he was seated next to them.

EVENTUALLY LADY EXNER took to her bed for an afternoon nap, which gave Regan a welcome break. She had hoped to sneak down to the next deck, where Luke and Nora had a first-class cabin, but after the episode of Veronica's near swan dive, decided not to leave her. Instead she stretched out in the chaise on the deck and reviewed the incredible events of the past forty-eight hours.

The realization that Athena had probably not caught the train to London that Friday night, but had been murdered right in Oxford, was beginning to fill her with guilt. Athena had asked her to come down to the pub next to the train station, the Bull and Bear, and have a drink before she caught her train. As the memory of those final moments came back in ever sharper focus, Regan thought, I almost went with her. But I didn't want to take the time. I was so glad she was leaving for a couple of days and I wouldn't have to listen to her nonstop complaining about St. Polycarp's and the English weather.

The ship was moving smoothly. The breeze was strong. Regan shivered and pulled on her sweatshirt. Livingston had asked her to try and remember anything at all that might be helpful in the investigation. Luke and Nora always teased her that she could remember everything from the time she was three. Regan laid back, closed her eyes, and from an investigative viewpoint began to recall the academic year she had spent in historic Oxford with Athena as her roommate.

Athena so seldom went to parties. She never indicated interest in any of the students. I never remember her going on a date, Regan thought. So who would want to kill her?

LUKE AND NORA spent a pleasant afternoon. After unpacking in the cabin they went to the sports deck for a drink and snack and then settled in deck chairs with their books.

"This is heaven," Nora murmured as she stared out, hypnotized by the sight of the open sea. "It's so nice to read somebody else's book instead of talking about one of mine."

She had been keynote speaker at a mystery convention in Spain and had followed that with an intense schedule of newspaper, magazine and television interviews in Italy and France.

Luke nodded, "Well, I've had enough of waiting in green rooms for a while." Then he frowned. "Speaking of green rooms, I wonder if Mrs. Shea is satisfied with the arrangements for Dennis. Maybe I'd better call and find out."

"Luke, it's not exactly a matter of life or death."

Luke chuckled as he enjoyed one of the oldest and, as Regan pointed out, corniest jokes they shared. "I see your point."

They returned to their books. Luke ordered another round of piña coladas and they remained comfortably ensconced until four-thirty, when the breeze turned sharply cooler. At that point there was a general flurry of activity as the occupants of the pool and scattered deck chairs began to gather their belongings, leaving the sports deck to the shuffleboard and paddle-tennis players.

As they meandered back to their cabin, they passed a group of children being led around the deck by two youth counselors. "It seems crazy to know Regan is on this ship and we have to avoid her," Nora said wistfully.

"Well, maybe we can get a table for four and you can spend the whole time taking notes for Lady Exner's totally authorized biography," Luke suggested.

"God forbid!" Nora exclaimed. "That reminds me. Regan warned me to make sure we're not sitting too near them in the dining room. Lady Eagle Eye might recognize me from my pictures on the book jackets."

The seating chart showed them to be in the nonsmoking section, well out of the view of anyone at Lady Exner's table.

"Regan's in the smoking section?" Nora said with not a little surprise in her voice. "I wonder if Lady Exner has shared that little jewel with her yet."

"She'll be all right," Luke observed. "Knowing Regan, after dinner she'll drag Lady Exner out for a walk on the deck to get some fresh air in her lungs."

"A moonlight stroll with an eighty-year-old woman," Nora lamented. "That Walker boy she was dating was so nice. If she'd only given him half a chance. I do so want to have a grand——"

"I know, I know," Luke interrupted. "Let's go."

GAVIN GRAY DRESSED for dinner carefully. It had been a tremendous relief to see Mrs. Watkins totter off the ship this morning, still wildly protesting the loss of her million-dollar bracelet. She had posted a reward of fifty thousand dollars, which had every steward, waiter and lackey walking around the ship with their eyes peeled, like a collection of hopeful lottery players waiting for their numbers to come up.

Don't waste your time, he had thought. I'm going to be the million-dollar winner. But there won't be any press conference to announce it. He deplored those idiotic television appearances of lottery winners surrounded by long-lost relatives with howdy-doody grins.

There was, of course, the obstacle of retrieving the bracelet from the Camelot Suite. He had already found out that a Lady Veronica Exner and her female companion would be staying there. It was good news that it was to be occupied by two women. The fear had lurked in the back of his mind that it would be inhabited on this crossing by a honeymooning couple who wouldn't come up for air until the skyline of New York City was in sight. But two women . . . He'd probably end up dancing with them anyway.

The first night out meant informal dress. Gavin laid out a pale yellow linen jacket and white slacks. His tie in place to his satisfaction, he pulled on his jacket and studied himself in the full-length mirror. Not bad, he reasoned. The facelift he'd had two years ago was still holding up. In fact, it looked even better.

That bargain-rate plastic surgeon had pulled the skin around his eyes so tight he could have blinded himself with dental floss.

The jacket hid his thickening waistline. Then he frowned. Its lemon-yellow tone accentuated the orangish shade of his just-colored hair. The girl at the salon on two deck had been too busy gossiping about the missing bracelet to notice the timer on the dryer had gone off. Gavin had dozed and by the time he woke up the dye had been on an extra twenty minutes. I look like a pumpkin head, he thought angrily. Oh shit, forget it. Next week I'll go to my hairdresser in New York. With that thought, a wave of anxiety washed over him. He was not booked as a host again until September. If he didn't retrieve the bracelet in these next few days, he wouldn't have another chance.

As he headed for the door of the cabin, he felt the undulating movement of the ship accelerate. Was it going to be another rough crossing? Then Gavin smiled. If so, maybe Lady Veronica Exner or her companion would need a steady arm to guide them back to the Camelot Suite.

AT 7 P.M., DRESSED in a lavender-and-white silk print by Mary Beth Downey, her favorite new designer, Regan sat waiting on the sofa which she had been thrilled to discover was indeed a pullout. Thank you, Bernadette Castro, she thought as she watched Veronica flutter around, trying on and rejecting various accessories. Regan had convinced Lady Exner that nobody dressed in formal evening wear the first night out. Reluctantly Veronica had abandoned the silver lamé ball gown in which she'd planned to make her grand entrance. Instead she settled for a simple blue crepe, one of the few items in her wardrobe that did not seem inspired by the drug culture.

With rapt attention Veronica again sprayed her already stiffened blond hair. Regan had been keeping count. That was the twelfth time in the last fifteen minutes. Regan was about to warn Veronica that it was getting late when Veronica reached for her purse. Regan stood up as Veronica squealed, "I almost forgot!"

"What is it, Veronica?" Regan asked anxiously. "Your medicine?"

"No. No. My cigarette holder." Veronica reached into the top drawer of the bureau and pulled out a leather case. She unzipped it and shook out a highly polished silver cigarette holder and an open pack of Benson & Hedges.

"Veronica, I've never seen you smoke."

"Of course I don't smoke. I simply give the appearance," Veronica answered gaily as she jammed a stale-looking cigarette into the holder.

Incredulous, Regan asked, "Why?"

"On our trips Penelope and I sit at a group table whenever possible. The nonsmokers' table is always filled with dreary reformed smokers who never want to have any fun. The people at the smokers' table have a reckless edge which I find intriguing."

Not a great commercial for the American Cancer Society, Regan thought as she tucked another allergy pill in her purse.

As they started down the hall to the small elevator which only served the two penthouses, the night steward approached them. Tall, stick-thin, with round glasses resting on a shiny nose and slicked-back brown hair, he looked to Regan like a college freshman. His voice had a hint of cockney as he asked if everything was satisfactory. After assuring him that it was, Veronica inquired about the occupants of the other suite. "I'm so anxious to meet them," Veronica bubbled. "Do you know who they are?"

The elevator arrived and the steward held the door open for them. "That suite is empty this crossing. You'll have total privacy up here." He released the door. "Enjoy your dinner."

AT FIVE MINUTES before seven o'clock, Cameron Hardwick was ready to leave for the cocktail lounge adjacent to the King Arthur Dining Room. He knew it was customary for many passengers to enjoy an aperitif before dinner, but in any case, everyone assigned to the King Arthur had to pass through the lounge. He wanted to be situated where he could follow Lady Exner into the dining room and place himself, if not actually next to her, as near as possible. The companion, he reflected, looked like she was in her mid to late twenties. Would it be smart to play up to her? Cameron considered. Maybe.

Carefully he examined his image in the mirror and frowned at the slight crease on his collar. Nobody knows how to do laundry anymore, he thought. At least the valet had done a decent job pressing his jacket and slacks. He liked to wear the seemingly ageless combination of a blue blazer, light blue shirt, striped tie and khaki pants. His Bally loafers had the gleam of shoes right out of the box. They weren't new but he was meticulous about every detail of his wardrobe.

He was ready to go. He gave one last admiring glance into the mirror at the deeply tanned good-looking guy he saw there. As always, the litany of praise he heard from women echoed through his head. The blonde at the croupier's table in Monaco who had slipped him her phone number while her boyfriend lost another hand of blackjack. "Don't ever stop scowling, Heathcliff," she'd purred. The rich college kid in London. "Boys my age are so immature. Not like you." The fiftyish widow he'd latched on to in Portugal. "It's no fun to go to the casinos alone. My husband was also tall and lean and handsome . . ."

He'd soaked in the gushing or whispered admiration while he escorted them to the high-stakes tables and later collected his share of their losses.

But for the last few years he'd realized that his own luck was subtly changing. He hadn't had a big win in too long. The women didn't mind paying for dinner or the suite, but they weren't as free with their cash anymore. He needed major bucks, the kind that would put that sense of being a winner back in his hands when he was dealt the cards. That was why, when this opportunity was presented to him, he'd grabbed it. It must be in the cards, he had thought. It's linked to my first bonanza.

The trophy of that first job was in the safe in his New York apartment. He'd only worn it once in public, that dazzling pocket watch with its equally beautiful fob, both encrusted with gemstones, ancient, priceless, created for a Doge of Venice in the sixteenth century. He had argued that it would be too dangerous to sell it anywhere, that it was on every list of stolen jewelry all over the world, that inevitably it would be traced back to him. Not true, of course. He wanted it for himself. He wanted to be able to put it on when he was alone, wear it with the brocaded dressing gown that closely resembled the ornate robes of a Doge and imagine that he was the master of Venice, the one who had built St. Mark's Cathedral as a private chapel.

Turning from the mirror, Cameron walked to the dresser, snapped on the Rolex watch that was a poor substitute for the hidden treasure, and reached for his card case. No, he thought as he put them back. I'm not handing these out to anyone on this ship. His cards, discreet, in exquisite taste with raised lettering on fine paperstock, gave his home address, 66 Gramercy Park South, New York City. No one need know he was in a rent-stabilized walk-up. He'd been smart enough technically to live with his father and never take a place of his own. The bitchy owners hadn't been able to repossess the apartment when the old drunk finally passed out for the last time. His occupation was listed as "personal investment counselor," which never failed to impress and which satisfied any curiosity about his lack of direct business commitment.

Cameron felt good. He was getting the sense he was on a winning streak. By the end of the trip two bodies would be bobbing around in the Atlantic. As he started for the cocktail lounge, he envisioned the moment when two hundred thousand dollars in cash was placed in his hand.

GAVIN GRAY ENTERED the cocktail lounge and looked around with an experienced eye. Not a very interesting group, he thought. There was the usual assortment of couples, some with the air of seasoned travellers, some overly dressed for first night, beaming with joy, overwhelmed by their good fortune at being one of the one-half of one percent of the people on earth who could afford to sail across the Atlantic. They'd probably never ridden anything bigger than the Staten Island ferry before, Gavin thought, dismissing them. It would be easy to avoid that type. They'd undoubtedly spend most of their time writing postcards that all started with "Wish you were here."

He was displeased to see that several tables in the lounge had been pushed together. A group of sixteen or so occupied them and already their laughter was becoming raucous. Gavin deplored the tendency of companies to reward their top salesmen with first-class cruises. There was something so essentially vulgar about brushing shoulders with people who were only on board because they had succeeded in unloading a quantity of snowmobiles or garage-door openers on gullible buyers. After all, when cruising really started in the 1920s, it was meant for the very elite who brought along their servants and were treated like royalty. He had voiced those thoughts to someone on the last crossing and his listener, a twentyish, leggy blonde, had said, "Well, at least they're paying. One of the ship's officers told me you have a free ride in exchange for dancing and playing bingo with blue-haired old ladies." Too late Gavin had found out that the leggy blonde was the daughter of the beefy head of the A-1 Sales Winners Club.

He ordered a gin and tonic and stood at the bar. There were three or four sets of harpies guzzling their vodkas. He recognized Sylvie Arden, the divorcée who had made countless crossings looking for a rich husband. Two trips ago she had confided that her cash was running pretty low. She had to get her hooks into someone pretty soon. Too frantic, my dear, Gavin sometimes warned her. Calm it a bit. You blitz when you should beguile. But he liked her. Sylvie was fun and they both understood each other. They surreptitiously compared notes on the old bats he jollied along and the old birds she tried to intrigue.

Gavin sighed. Back to work, he decided. He had noticed a table where two sixtyish women were eyeing the crowd with avid glances. Rhett Butler can't make it, ladies, he thought as he drifted over to chat with them. He stopped abruptly when he saw the couple who were standing in the doorway of the lounge. Surely. Of course it was. Nora Regan Reilly. There was no mistaking her. That small trim figure, that pretty face, the ash-blond hair, short and wavy. She'd been on his program several times and had been one of the last guests he'd had just before it was canceled a year ago. And that was her husband, the funeral director. Talk about a lousy job! Gavin rushed to greet them, immediately assuming his talk-show persona. "Nora Regan Reilly," he boomed.

"Ssshhh." Panic-stricken, Nora and Luke whirled their heads around. They had spotted Regan and Lady Exner stepping off the elevator and rushed to put a healthy distance between them. Of all the luck to meet Gabby Gavin, Nora thought. I'll never have any privacy on this trip. And, oh God, here they come.

Regan and Lady Exner were less than six feet away. Regan caught Nora's eye and began making frantic shooing motions with her hand. Fortunately Lady Exner had paused to light a cigarette and all her attention was devoted to the lighter, whose starter was clearly not responding to her vigorous thumb-snapping.

Luke took Gavin's arm and propelled him to an isolated table. "We've got something to let you in on," he explained in a low voice.

They told it straight. Their daughter was on board acting as a companion to an elderly woman, Lady Veronica Exner, whose goal in life was to have Nora collaborate on her memoirs. For that reason they wanted no one to identify Mrs. Luke Reilly as mystery writer Nora Regan Reilly.

"I'm sure she's a lovely person," Nora said, "but we really took this cruise to unwind and be together."

Gavin was sure he had died and gone to heaven. Nora Regan Reilly's daughter was Lady Exner's companion! And they were staying in the Camelot Suite. It would be so easy to get friendly with them. His thoughts moved with lightning speed. "I certainly understand your dilemma. My celebrity friends all cherish their privacy."

Celebrity friends, Nora thought. The only people he's interested in. You'd think he'd hosted "The Tonight Show" instead of his dinky radio broadcast which had had about three listeners. Once she'd been on and he'd spent half the time begging the audience to call in with questions. Luke and Regan had spent the whole half hour trying to find it on the dial. In vain, of course. And as for privacy, forget it. He couldn't help himself. He loved to name drop.

Now Gavin hunched over the table and his eye disappeared in a lengthy conspiratorial wink. "It will be our little secret," he assured them. "As a matter of fact, I believe I'm seated at their table. Do tell your daughter that I'll be happy to accompany Lady Exner to some of the activities. There's a psychic on board who invariably attracts senior citizens to her sessions. Why, I'll never know." Gavin drained his glass and broke out his hearty show-business laugh. "Her specialty is predicting the future, and since many of them look as though they won't live to see land again, her predictions should be limited to which selection on the dinner menu will be easiest to chew." He stood up. "She should really predict when they'll be needing the services of someone like you, huh, Luke?"

No, Luke thought. You're the only stiff around here.

I DON'T NEED any more close calls like that, Regan thought, and I don't want to be around when the maître d' discovers that Veronica's cigarette singed the back of his jacket when he leaned over to look up our table number.

"Beautiful ladies, follow me," he smiled.

Three people were already seated at the spacious round table: a middle-aged couple who offered a big welcome, and a rail-thin fashionably dressed frosted blonde who could have been anywhere between fifty and sixty. She was situated opposite the couple. Good move, Regan thought. No doubt the single woman had left plenty of empty seats around her hoping they'd be filled by that rare commodity on cruise ships, single men.

The maître d' seated Veronica and pulled out the chair to her left for Regan.

General introductions followed. Mario and Immaculata Buttacavola announced they were taking their first cruise ever, and had decided to go all out by traveling first class. "The way I see it," Mario explained, "I work for a swank hotel in Atlantic City and figured it's high time me and the missus got a taste of the good life. Besides, being I'm in the banquet office, maybe I can earn some Brownie points by bringing back new ideas about ship-style food and beverage service. Everyone tells me all you do on a cruise is eat." He patted his generous girth. "I'm ready."

Immaculata gazed at him with an adoring look that made Nancy Reagan's swoonlike gaze at Ron seem surly. "This is like a second honeymoon for us," she bubbled.

Sylvie Arden was from Palm Springs. "I love to travel," she

sighed, "but I hate packing and unpacking. That's why cruising is the perfect solution for me. You unpack once and then just enjoy yourself."

"Good evening."

Regan and the others turned to see a sophisticated-looking dark-haired man in his late thirties approach. Sylvie's eyes brightened as he chose the seat between her and Veronica. "May I?" he asked.

"Please do!" Veronica and Sylvie chorused.

A moment later the seat to the left of Regan was filled. A man about her father's age wearing a lemon jacket introduced himself as Gavin Gray and greeted the frosted blonde with the familiarity of old friends.

"So good to see you, Sylvie," he said.

"You two know each other?" Veronica cried as she waved the cigarette holder, whipping it past Regan's nose.

"Oh yes," Gavin replied. "We've been on many of these sea adventures together. You see, I am originally from Manhattan. For many years I was the host of "Gavin's Guests," a popular radio program in New York. I interviewed literally thousands of celebrities. Now that I am retired, I have taken my interest in people into an affiliation with the cruise line. I am one of your hosts."

Gavin Gray, Regan thought. Gavin Gray. I've heard his name. Of course! She'd been in New York when Nora was on that program. Nora called him Gabby Gavin and said she doubted he ever read a book before he interviewed the author. Regan's heart sank. If he spotted Nora and talked about her to Veronica, that would be it.

The dark-haired man on Veronica's right volunteered, "I'm Cameron Hardwick from New York." His smile was pleasant.

Veronica spoke for Regan and herself. "I am Lady Veronica Exner from Oxford, widow of the late Sir Gilbert Exner, and this is my dear friend, Regan Reilly."

Immaculata Buttacavola's large brown eyes filled with understanding. "Did you lose your husband recently?" she asked tenderly.

"Forty years ago," Veronica said briskly, but then added, "sometimes it feels like yesterday."

Oh brother, Regan thought. Let's hope Immaculata what's-her-name doesn't ask Veronica how long they were married.

"Regan Reilly," Gavin Gray mused. "What a charming name." He gave her a knowing look and a hint of a wink.

The captain, pad in hand, approached them. "Do you care to order a beverage now?"

"Lovely." It was obvious that Veronica had already become the self-appointed spokesperson. "But tell me. Will these two seats be occupied?" Her question was hopeful.

Regan couldn't help but notice that Sylvie Arden was trembling to hear the answer.

"Yes, they certainly will," called out one of two men circling the table and heading for the empty seats. He was about five feet nine, of average build, with thinning brown hair flecked with gray, a matching mustache, and horn-rimmed glasses that magnified amused, intelligent eyes. His companion was a couple of inches taller, a bit stockier, and his shiny black hair was pulled back into a ponytail fastened by a diamond clip. Both seemed to be in their early forties.

Regan watched Sylvie's hopes dry up faster than a drop of water on a sizzling sidewalk as she realized that the newcomers were a couple.

"Oh, perfect timing," Veronica gushed. "We're just about to order our sherry."

"I'm not having sherry," Mario protested.

"It gives him a headache," Immaculata rushed to explain. "We usually have a mixed drink before dinner. It could be a tequila sunrise, it could be a rye and ginger, it could be an old-fashioned; on special occasions I get out the blender and start to make—"

"Could we possibly place our orders?" Cameron Hardwick interrupted, a hint of impatience in his voice.

The first of the new arrivals was seated next to Immaculata. Quickly he turned to her, smiling warmly. "Your suggestion of an old-fashioned is marvelous. Will you join us in one? Does that sound good to you, Kenneth?''

The moment of tension passed as they gave their orders. You're a nice guy, Regan thought, smiling across the table at the newcomer. And what about you, Cameron Hardwick? she wondered. You're good-looking, well-dressed, and at an age when a lot of women should be chasing after you and you're traveling alone? Why? You must be a prick.

The introductions began again. Regan was relieved that on this go-round everyone just volunteered their names. The late arrivals went last.

''I'm Dale Cohoon,'' said the one with the glasses who had done all the talking, ''and this is my friend, Kenneth Minard.''

''Nice to meet you all.'' As he patted his hair behind his ears and adjusted his cuffs, Kenneth favored them with a nervous smile. ''All this rushing. Dale and I were out on the deck working on our tans and were both so exhausted, we fell dead asleep. We didn't have nearly enough time to get dressed for dinner properly.''

''Poor Kenneth.'' Dale's tone was loving and sympathetic. ''I've dragged him all over Europe hunting down antiques for my shop. We live in San Francisco.''

''Antiques!'' Veronica's eyes brightened. ''I adore browsing through antique shops.''

Browse must be all you do, Regan thought. From the looks of Llewellyn Hall, the only real antique is the plumbing system.

''And what is your profession, Kenneth?'' Veronica inquired.

She could sub for Barbara Walters, Regan thought.

''I'm a hair stylist,'' Kenneth told her proudly.

The drinks arrived. Cameron Hardwick began to chat with Lady Exner. Gavin Gray was listening to Mario's and Immaculata's questions about the activities on the ship. Regan glanced around, enjoying the gentle sway of the ship as it gracefully moved through the night. The room was decorated in a blue-green motif that suggested the ocean setting. Huge windows ran from floor to ceiling on both the port and starboard sides. The moon was bright and glistened on the dark murky sea. The tables were now filled, and captains and waiters bustled as they took orders and carried silver-covered dishes. The sommelier, wearing an impressive key around his neck, was opening a bottle of Dom Perignon with theatrical flair. At tables for two, some couples were smiling, others looked as though they had run out of conversation twenty years ago. A strolling violinist was winding his way through the room, his bow planted firmly under his chin. What do violinists with small chins do? Regan wondered. Endure a lifetime of neck pain?

She looked over her shoulder. From where she was sitting she could not spot Luke and Nora. "They're at the corner table behind the pillar," Gavin Gray whispered.

Regan stared at him. "Excuse me."

His eye once again disappeared into a squiggly line. "I'm a dear friend of your mother and father," he hissed. "I had a drink with them in the lounge and understand the predicament. It will be our little secret." He grabbed her hand and squeezed it. His second wink made Regan wonder whether he was working his way into a nervous tic. She managed to withdraw her hand. She tried to wink back but it felt ridiculous.

"Regan, do you have something in your eye?" Veronica asked.

"No, I'm fine." Regan anxiously reached for her glass of wine. I only hope I can trust him, she thought.

The captain took the dinner orders. Regan, Lady Exner and Gabby decided on the coq au vin as the main course. Kenneth and Dale ordered the rack of lamb. Cameron and Sylvie decided on the steak au poivre. Mario and Immaculata had a terrible time choosing between the lamb and the steak. They finally agreed to order one of each and share. They also ordered onion soup. When the waiter was about to make his escape Mario pulled him back and said, "You may as well give us some of them crab-meat appetizers."

Throughout the meal the conversation varied between group talk and individual exchanges. Sylvie Arden bounced back from her initial disappointment at the slim pickings of eligible men and spoke knowledgeably with Dale Cohoon about Regency furniture. Except for his grunts of contentment, Mario didn't say a word during the meal. He meticulously mopped up every trace of liquid on his plate with a sour-dough roll.

Kenneth listened with admirable patience to Immaculata's description of her adorable grandchildren, Concepcione, "who is sort of named after me," and Mario the Third, "the image of his father." She ordered big Mario to pull out his wallet and pass their pictures around. Regan smiled and murmured polite compliments about the two chubby-cheeked toddlers.

Veronica was too busy trying to light yet another stale cigarette to do more than glance at the snapshots of the youngest Buttacavolas. She passed them on to Cameron Hardwick, who looked visibly pained and fired the collection at Sylvie. A waiter rushed to assist Veronica, who huffed and puffed until a dismal glow at the tip of the cigarette rewarded her efforts. With that accomplished, Veronica launched into a rhapsody of how the late Sir Gilbert had always enjoyed coq au vin. She went on to describe his life and times in minute detail, proclaiming him a Renaissance man who wrote beautiful poetry. When she finally ran out of breath Sylvie quickly changed the subject by asking Gavin if the missing bracelet from the last crossing had turned up.

"Not that I know of," Gavin said, sounding a touch abrupt.

"One of the stewards was telling me all about it," Sylvie confided. "I've made several crossings with Mrs. Watkins. She wears so much jewelry she looks like Queen for a Day. But that bracelet she lost was really something. They've posted a fifty-thousand-dollar reward for whoever finds it."

"What happened?" Veronica asked, sounding excited.

"Gavin, you were there. You tell," Sylvie replied.

"Well, I was on the ship," Gavin answered with a defensive tone, then quickly resumed the demeanor of a genial host. "Apparently it fell off her wrist. It was the night of the Captain's party. Who knows? Anyone could have picked it up."

"From what the steward tells me, they ripped the ship apart looking for it," Sylvie insisted. "Mrs. Watkins travels frequently on this line," she explained to everyone at the table. "I must have met her a dozen times. She spends money like water and always books the Camelot Suite."

"That's where we're staying," Veronica cried. "Regan and I are all alone up there. I was hoping we'd have neighbors, but the suite across the hall is empty." She puffed on her cigarette. "I'll have to keep my eye out for the hidden treasure."

"The steward is convinced that bracelet went off the ship in someone's luggage," Sylvie continued. "They're sure whoever found it kept it. I know it was worth a fortune, but I thought it was awfully garish."

"Antique jewelry is the only jewelry worth having," Cameron Hardwick commented. "The real craftsmen died a couple of hundred years ago."

"I have a friend who deals in antique jewelry who agrees with you," Dale said. "Do you collect?"

"I have one or two interesting pieces," Hardwick replied with a knowing smile.

It was only after Mario and Immaculata had finished their horn of plenty, a dessert described on the menu as "a symphony of fresh fruit in puff pastry on raspberry sauce," and were sipping their cappuccino that Immaculata jumped back into the conversation, picking up where Sylvie had left off.

"There's nothing worse than being robbed. Such an invasion. Last year when we were visiting Mario Junior and Roz and the children—they live about twenty miles from us—we ended up staying the night. It was an act of God that the car didn't start. Mario Junior offered to lend us his car but it has a stick shift and big Mario hasn't driven one of those in thirty years. So we ended up staying in the guest room. That way we could get the car fixed in the morning and be on our way. The munchkins love it when we stay over. That very night our own home was robbed. My neighbor noticed a car parked in front at around eleven o'clock. That was exactly the time we would have arrived if our car had started. Who knows? We could have walked in on them and been killed. I knew something was wrong the minute we pulled in the driveway and there were Mario's old dentures on the welcome mat. His new ones don't snap in quite as good, so he keeps the old pair for around the house. They were in his jewelry box with his good cuff links and his solid-gold watch, and you know what? We figured the robbers must have had good teeth and didn't need them." She laughed heartily at her own witticism.

"And they took all my jewelry, the ring big Mario gave me when Mario Junior was born, they took cash and silver . . ." She shook her head. "But I still say if Roz hadn't made us stay . . . The car actually started to turn over and stopped. Mario was going to try it again. But Roz said, 'If it dies on the highway in this rain, you could have an accident.' She didn't want us to go back. And I think she saved our lives. Terrible, terrible. Did you know that one out of every four people in the United States will be the victim of a crime in their lifetime?"

Regan had been about to blurt out the correct statistics, if only to stem the flow of Immaculata's narrative, but clamped her lips just in time. On this voyage Regan thought it best to avoid talking about her occupation.

The sommelier was at the table. "Would anyone care for a cordial or a liqueur?"

With one voice, Kenneth, Dale, Sylvie, Cameron and Gavin said no, almost knocking their chairs over as they jumped up. Veronica agreed to join the Buttacavolas for a crème de menthe.

Regan wondered how many miles they were from the Hudson River.

AFTER DINNER CAMERON Hardwick fled onto the deck. He'd had about all he could stand of Mario and Immaculata oohing and aahing over every bite of food or violin selection. He'd also had enough of that old windbag waving that damn cigarette holder past his face. The ashes had landed in both his salad and soup before she'd finally put it down and attacked her own dinner.

He hoped that when the moment came to get rid of her, she'd have that holder and those butts in her pocket and they'd disappear with her.

The night breeze was strong. A few people were walking arm in arm on the deck, but most women, Cameron noticed, turned back immediately when they felt the chilling draft. Don't want to get their hair mussed, he thought contemptuously as he paused to fold his arms over the railing and study the dark water with the churning foam slapping the side of the ship. Then from his left he heard a now familiar voice.

"And Regan, dear, no matter how brisk, on land or at sea, I never miss getting in my daily walk. Inhale that wonderful pungent scent. It bespeaks milleniums of tides, rising and falling. I have always loved that poem, 'I Must Go Down to the Sea Again.' "

"Veronica, I like to walk too. But let's run upstairs and get you a jacket."

"Look, look. Here is dear Cameron Hardwick. Regan, if you insist, go get my jacket. I'll wait with Cameron and we can chat."

Hardwick felt a hand on his arm. With all the charm he

could muster, he patted her freckled fingers. "What a pleasant surprise." He wondered if Reilly could read his mind. Even in the dark he could see that she was studying him.

"I don't like to leave Lady Exner alone out here," she told him. "Veronica, I really wish—"

"She'll be fine." Hardwick tried to sound reassuring. "In fact, I think we should keep walking. We'll go to the bow and then turn around. We'll stay on this side of the deck."

Veronica's arm was now firmly planted in his. "Such a strong man," she flirted.

"You're flattering me, Lady Exner," he said in what he hoped was a bantering tone.

"But it's true. Dear Gilbert was a rather frail person. A giant intellect but a distressingly troubled body. Run along, Regan," she ordered imperiously. "I'm well protected by dear Mr. Hardwick."

Regan reasoned to herself, he doesn't seem to mind. I'll only be gone for five minutes and he's certainly capable of hanging on to her for that long. And if I don't get her a jacket, she'll end up on a respirator in Sickbay. "As long as it's no trouble . . ." she said and ducked back into the lounge.

"Such a dear girl and such a worrier," Veronica told him as they began to move toward the bow. "And such an interesting table we have. Dear Mr. Gavin has offered to escort me to the Sit-and-Be-Fit session tomorrow morning. Dear Mr. Cohoon is going to give me some ideas for sprucing up Llewellyn Hall. He offered to stop by on his next London trip, which will be in September. I intend to ask dear Mr. Kenneth's advice about my hairdo. I've been wearing it like this for four years and maybe it's time for a change. I'm afraid the couple may become a bit tiresome with their anecdotes about their grandchildren, but probably on the return crossing I'll be a fountain of anecdotes about my nieces. I long to see them and make them part of the family. Philip, my nephew, is a sweet impractical darling, but a woman rather wants a daughter, don't you think? And while Philip's fiancée is a wonder—so efficient, so thoughtful—I have the feeling that I get on her nerves. But then, blood is thicker than water, isn't it?"

By now they were the only two people on this side of the deck. It was dark. Lady Exner couldn't weigh more than ninety pounds. In an instant he could punch her into a daze to prevent an outcry, then toss her overboard. When Regan Reilly came back he could claim that Exner had gone in to use the ladies' room, then get rid of her the same way. Who would suspect him? They'd just met. He'd come alone. Reilly and Exner had come out onto the deck alone . . .

Should he? . . .

Yes.

The perfect opportunity didn't repeat itself. They were at the darkest point of the deck. Cameron drew back his free hand.

And heard footsteps.

Across the bow, from the starboard side of the ship, a couple was approaching. He could hear their voices before he saw their silhouettes.

"Nora, you're not dressed warmly enough. Let's go back inside."

As they came closer Hardwick saw that it was the same couple he had followed onto the ship this morning. When they saw him and Lady Exner standing at the rail, they turned wordlessly and retreated.

The moment had passed. It had also taught Cameron that there was no way he could risk trying to get rid of Lady Exner and Regan Reilly on a public deck. He would have to find another solution.

VERONICA AND REGAN stopped at the small piano bar for a nightcap on their way back to the suite. "I need a little something to chase the chill from my bones, dear Regan, and I think a nip of Scotch would do the trick." Veronica grabbed seats surrounding the piano and grew misty-eyed as the tuxedo-clad musician played selections from *Phantom of the Opera*. "Sir Gilbert would have loved that show," she whispered in Regan's ear.

A half hour later, after Veronica had made requests for "I Love You, Truly," and "Memory," they returned to their quarters, where the steward had already turned down the beds.

"The arms of Morpheus should have plenty of room for both of us tonight," Veronica crowed, "and since I haven't gotten any other offers, Mr. M will have to do."

It was at that moment that Regan knew that Veronica had indeed succeeded in chasing the chill from her body. As Regan undressed and moved in and out of the bathroom, Veronica continued her monologue, undeterred by the sound of the faucet running.

"And do say a prayer for dear Gilbert. I must admit he was a bit of an agnostic, but he did make an annual contribution to the Church of England and always sent the local minister a Christmas offering."

Regan walked up the three steps to the living room area and gratefully got under the sheets in her own bed, wondering how Veronica had managed to learn so much about Sir Gilbert during their two-week marriage.

Veronica's prayers for Sir Gilbert must have been right to the point. About thirty seconds after her head hit the pillow, the snores began. As a snore pattern, it was rather unique, Regan found herself thinking. A short bark followed by a watery gurgle that reminded her she was due for a teeth cleaning.

Regan hunched and twisted and tried to get herself into a comfortable position. These pillows are too thick, she thought as she punched them with her fist. But they'd be perfect for Dad's clients, she mumbled as she lay back down, yet was still involuntarily propped up. Pulling them out from under her head, she leaned them against her ears, ensconcing herself in a tiny fort in an effort to dull the cacophony emanating from the king-sized bed.

Usually she could drop off to sleep quickly, but tonight her mind refused to slow down. The first day was over and she totally understood why Philip had insisted that Veronica must not travel alone. If Regan had not been there, Veronica would have plunged from the railing. For the next four and a half days, until she delivered her to her niece, either Regan or someone she could trust would have to stick close to Veronica's side.

Oddly, it was not so much the eventful day she had just completed that was on her mind, but scenes from the weekend at Oxford, which kept insisting themselves into her thoughts. The way she and Kit had joked about Athena. Her own belief that ten years ago Athena had chosen not to come back to school. It was as though she could feel Athena's presence, hear Athena's rapid, emotion-charged, accented voice. I want to call Livingston, Regan thought, and find out if there's anything new. But it's too late to do it tonight.

Crouched in a fetal position, Veronica slept the night away. For hours, Regan lay awake staring wide-eyed at the terrace, watching the constantly evolving shadows as the ship glided through the Atlantic. She shut her eyes briefly, then opened them again and saw a shadow that resembled a human silhouette framed in the terrace door. She bolted up and felt her pulse leaping as her breath caught in her throat. In a split second the moon moved from behind the clouds and the shadow disappeared. Regan shuddered. She who was almost never nervous had experienced an instant of pure terror. She swallowed quickly. Was that what it was like for Athena in the last minutes of her life? Tears stung her eyes.

Who could have killed her? The local papers in Greece were undoubtedly having a field day with Athena's death, especially because it happened only eight months after her aunt's murder. Two members of a wealthy, prominent family dying violently was the stuff that sold papers. Maybe if I could read a transcript of what is being written in the Greek media, it might remind me of something I've overlooked, Regan thought suddenly. She decided that when she called Livingston in the morning she would ask him to get newspaper accounts from Greece translated and faxed to her on the ship. The prospect was comforting. At least it was a start.

She finally fell into a troubled sleep in which, in her dreams, the creaks and groans of the ship were transformed into the sound of footsteps pursuing her. It was Veronica who awakened her at 8 A.M.

"Wake up, sleepyhead. Oh, how I wish I could sleep with the abandon of the young. I scarcely closed an eye all night."

Regan opened her eyes to find Veronica already dressed in an orange-and-white-striped jumpsuit with a matching headband.

"Directly after breakfast they have the Sit-and-Be-Fit class. I can't wait to meet the people in it. Hurry and get ready. We'll go down to the Lido Deck for coffee and rolls. I don't want to waste a minute of this adventure."

Regan showered quickly, her half-remembered dreams and churning thoughts about Athena foremost in her mind. She felt as though she were in a long corridor with many doors and didn't know which one to open. She wished she could talk it through with Jeff. Sometimes using him as a sounding board clarified her own thoughts.

When she opened the bathroom door, she nearly ran into Veronica, who had been ready to pound on it.

"Don't take such long showers, Regan. It's very drying on your lovely young skin. And now let's be off. Our public awaits us."

Tuesday, June 23, 1992

GAVIN GRAY DID not enjoy a fulsome night's sleep. Visions of a diamond-and-emerald bracelet danced in his dreams. When he recovered it, and redeemed it, he would have at least a million dollars. Tax-free. Decently invested, that could mean an income of ninety thousand dollars a year. For that he could rent a château and live like a king on the Costa del Sol in Spain. Far away from the likes of Veronica Exner and old Mrs. Watkins, not to mention the Buttinskys or whatever the hell their name was. He would never have to lay eyes on another Bingo card ever again.

At 6:30 A.M., as the sun filtered through the fog, Gavin got up, showered, and dressed in a sweat suit. He decided to go to the buffet breakfast by the pool. That way he could be sure to eat quickly. He needed several cups of strong coffee before he could face contorting himself like a monkey with Veronica Exner and her fellow relics in the Sit-and-Be-Fit class.

It was a good decision. He carefully placed coffee, freshly squeezed orange juice and a warm, flaky croissant onto a tray and carried it to a table near the railing. The breeze was cool and the tangy scent of salt blew away the headache that had been threatening to develop. Looking out at the blue-green ocean with the flecks of white foam on the swells, Gavin found himself amazed again at the ship's aloneness. The vast plain of water that lapped at its sides stretched out for miles undisturbed by any other signs of life. Gavin took a sip of his juice. Hard to believe that right now barges all over were probably dumping tons of garbage into its depths of the ocean.

Fortified by his second cup of coffee, Gavin checked his watch. It was time to head for the lounge where the Sit-and-Be-Fit class was to be held. His timing was perfect. Regan Reilly and Lady Exner were just entering the lounge from the opposite door. Gavin noticed that Lady Exner looked overwhelmingly bright-eyed, whereas Miss Reilly looked as if she could use a little more sleep. After a hearty good morning he took Lady Exner's arm possessively and dismissed Regan with a wink, assuring her that all would be well.

As the instructor clapped his hands and called "Places, everyone," Regan exited the lounge. When she'd been in the shower she'd made a quick call to Luke and Nora from the bathroom phone and knew they'd be waiting for her in their cabin.

NORA AND LUKE were enjoying a leisurely breakfast in the sitting room of their suite. There was an extra place set and with a sigh of relief Regan sat down as Nora poured coffee into the waiting cup. Nora was wearing a pink silk robe and Regan thought appreciatively how good she looked without makeup. Luke was already dressed in a navy blue sweat suit which on him somehow looked formal.

The suite was decorated in tones of ivory and peach. The sun poured through the large portholes and Regan felt herself begin to relax. "I've got exactly forty-five minutes before I collect Veronica," she announced.

"How's it going, honey?" Nora asked with an amused expression.

"This reminds me of going out on a first date and within ten minutes you know you've made a big mistake and are in for a long evening."

"The problem seems to be that this first date is of five days' duration," Luke volunteered.

"Thanks, Dad. I thought you were in the business of offering comfort." Regan yawned. "Veronica is a handful. She had a party for us this weekend that really turned into something unexpected. Do you remember my roommate, Athena, from Saint Polycarp's?"

"Black fingernails?" Nora murmured. "She eloped or something?"

"The 'or something' is that she was murdered," Regan said. As they listened, their expressions shocked, she sketched the details of the discovery of Athena's body. "Superintendent Livingston asked me to try to remember anything Athena might have told me about plans to meet someone. I drew an absolute blank but I'm going to get my journal out of the attic at home and see if that helps and I also have another idea . . ." Regan told them about her plan to call Livingston and ask him to fax her newspaper accounts from Greece about Athena's death.

"That's a smart move," Nora said thoughtfully. "It's like an investigator picking up the file of an unsolved crime years later and seeing something he missed on the first go-round."

Regan placed the ship-to-shore call from their phone. As she waited for the connection to go through, she sat down on the loveseat. "Let me know how much this costs. I just don't want it on Veronica's account."

Nora and Luke both smiled. "Sure, we'll bill you," Luke drawled. "And incidentally, you had two cups of coffee, one orange juice and half a bran muffin."

Regan was eyeing the clock nervously when the operator rang back to say she had Superintendent Livingston on the line. Quickly Regan identified herself and explained her proposal regarding the Greek newspapers.

"I'll get them to you directly," the Inspector told her. "We can have them translated quickly, and possibly there's an English-language newspaper in the area of the family home. We ourselves have come up with nothing helpful. But there is something else you should know. Miss Atwater had a narrow escape. She will recover, but traces of poison were found in her system."

"Penelope was poisoned?" Regan gripped the receiver, not believing what she had just heard. "But how?"

Livingston's tone became cautious. "Apparently she made a paste for biscuits to serve at Lady Exner's cocktail party. From what she tells us she finished the last of the lot in her room Sunday night. The maid found a piece of one of them crumpled in her bedcovers. Rather reminds one of the saying, 'You can eat crackers in my bed anytime.' Oh dear. When the poison was found in her system we immediately began an investigation and were fortunate in that she's a bit of an untidy lady, I gather, and therefore the crumbs."

"Is it possible she made a mistake and put something in the paste herself?" Regan asked.

"Most people don't store arsenic on the pantry shelf," Livingston observed. "Very odd, this whole business. I'll get any news clippings faxed to you straightaway and certainly hope they are helpful in jogging your memory."

Regan hung up. Hurriedly she filled Luke and Nora in on what had happened to Penelope, then said, "I've got to get back. Gabby Gavin is bringing Veronica up to the suite, and the boat drill starts in fifteen minutes."

As she darted out the door, Nora called after her, "Regan, I'm worried. Athena's body was found near the Exner estate and this Penelope woman was poisoned there. For God's sake, be careful!"

"TIGHTEN THOSE BUTTOCKS. And hold. And one and two and three. Now release and two and three. And squeeze and two and hard, harder and release . . ."

Gavin looked around. These people could sit here from now till Doomsday squeezing their buns but they still won't end up with tight asses. Sit-and-Be-Fit. What a joke. It was like telling a couch potato he was building up his muscles by pushing the remote control with one hand and lifting a Twinkie to his mouth with the other. But from the looks on the faces of all the oldsters surrounding Gavin, it was obvious they thought something worthwhile was going on. Maybe it was all that squeezing.

Forty-five minutes later the young muscle man instructor yelled "Thank youuuuu, alllll," as he clapped his hands enthusiastically. "See you tomorrow and watch out for all that fattening food they serve all day long. And have fun! Go out and get some of that sea air!"

"I will. I will," Veronica cried out. "But first we must all prepare for the boat drill." That proclamation having fallen on the ears of her fellow exercisers, who shook their heads in agreement and muttered "Oh yess, um hmmm, that's right," Veronica jumped to her feet. "Gavin, I'll race you back to the suite." In a shot she was off.

Gavin hoisted his not overweight yet not fit body out of the chair and ran after her. Veronica's course followed a zigzag path as her body veered starboard and then port and then back to starboard, through the maze of corridors and staircases, in tune with the creaking and leaning of the ship. Just as she was reaching the door he caught her arm. "Lady Exner, I have a tough time keeping up with you." He forced a laugh. This woman is going to put me in my grave, he thought. Either that or drive me crazy.

"Exercise releases endorphins which gives one a sense of well-being and energy which begets energy. It's just like the smashing feeling of being in love that eating chocolate can re-create. Which reminds me. I've got a Mars bar which I'll split with you." She smiled up at him.

Maybe my ex-wife Clovis wasn't so bad after all, Gavin thought.

As they entered the suite Gavin's heart started to pound even harder. Maybe I'll have a chance to nab the bracelet, he thought. It was only Tuesday but if the opportunity presented itself . . .

"Excuse me, but as they say at sea, I must use the head," Veronica blushed. Tittering, she shut the bathroom door.

Gavin stood there, not believing his own luck. He looked around and spotted the small stool in front of the vanity in the bedroom area. This was his chance. That jump suit Lady Exner was wearing would probably take a few minutes to peel off and a couple more to yank back on.

He hurried over, grabbed the stool with both hands and dashed up the steps to the closet. Ha! It was natural for him to get the life preservers out for her. They were within easy reach but he knew he'd shoved the bracelet so far back on the top shelf he'd have to stand on something to get it. Which of course would look fishy even to a dingbat like Lady Exner.

Opening the closet door, he was once again subject to the mean stare of the orange water wings. I never should have thrown the bracelet on that top shelf, he thought angrily. He pulled the stool in closer and, carefully balancing himself, placed both feet on the cushion usually reserved for wealthy rumps. Grabbing the doorframe, he pulled himself up at the same moment the sound of the toilet flushing announced Lady Exner's imminent return. He reached up and fumbled for the bracelet when the toilet whooshed again and he heard Regan Reilly's voice outside the door, chatting with the steward, as she placed her key in the lock.

Not close enough to locate his hidden treasure, he jumped back down and frantically shut the door, ran over to the couch with the stool, dropped it, and stretched his left leg out on top.

"Regan, you are just in time. Mr. Gray is here to give us personal instructions for the boat drill. He is so kind." As Veronica walked up to the living room she added, "Oh dear, is there something wrong with your leg?"

"I guess all the squeezing got to me. I seem to have aggravated an old hamstring injury I sustained when I was water skiing out in the Hamptons at a big celebrity party. I'll be fine."

Regan wondered if this was a first. She couldn't imagine there were too many people besides Gabby Gavin who could walk away from a Sit-and-Be-Fit class in pain. "We may as well get suited up," Regan said brightly. "Let's get out those life jackets."

CAMERON HARDWICK WAS not pleased to see that Gavin Gray was at the same lifeboat station where he was assigned. Hardwick deliberately stayed at the edge of the group, bored with the nervous giggling of his fellow passengers as they tightened the straps on each other's life jackets and told stories of people they knew who were on a ship that had to be evacuated. Some idiot started singing "Nearer My God to Thee" in honor of the *Titanic* but finally shut up after a withering glance from the officer in charge who droned on about emergency procedures.

Gray was standing near the officer and Hardwick had a good chance to study him. His eyes narrowed as he realized Gray was flushed and a nervous tic was jumping under his eye. Something's really gotten to him, Hardwick thought and wondered what it could be. This morning, Hardwick had observed Lady Exner and Regan Reilly in the breakfast area from across the deck, and from a distance had followed them to the lounge. When it became clear that Gavin Gray was going to stick with Exner for the exercise class, he'd left. Now, as he continued to study Gray's distracted, tense face, his curiosity turned to annoyance. He knew what Gray was. One of those professional escorts ships hire to dance with the old hens. But that job certainly didn't include Gray's swinging his butt around in an exercise class. What was his big interest in Exner, and was he going to be another problem? Cameron decided it was time to get his hands on a key to Exner's suite, and to the empty one across the hall. Quietly he slipped away from the lifeboat station and into the lounge. As he had hoped, it was deserted. Careful to be sure he wasn't being observed, he made his way to the stairs and up to the top deck. The silence when he reached it convinced him that the on-duty steward was at the drill. Hardwick walked noiselessly to the small room that served as the steward's station just down the hall and around the bend from Lady Exner's suite. The door was unlocked. He slipped in, his eyes darting from desk to chair to file cabinet to the wall panel that would light up for room service.

Cameron went through the desk drawers. They were a somewhat untidy jumble of lists and regulations, paper clips and pens, crumbs and candy. The bottom drawer held a pint of Jack Daniels. Cameron lifted his eyebrows. A steward who imbibed on duty was probably pretty careless. Hopefully it's the night steward who likes to drink.

He went to the file cabinet. As he had hoped, it was unlocked. There were only about a dozen files but in the last one he found what he was seeking. A key ring with three spare keys for the two suites. He helped himself to one of each of them.

As he left the steward's station he heard the whir of the elevator. The staircase was at the end of the long corridor. He would not have time to get to it without being seen. With giant strides he ran to the door of the unoccupied suite and let himself in. He was just closing it when he heard Lady Exner's high-pitched voice telling Regan Reilly how perfectly thrilling the drill had been.

Hardwick leaned against the door and let out a silent whistle. If Reilly had seen him up here, alarms would have gone off in her head. He'd taken a chance but feeling the keys in his hand made it worthwhile.

The draperies were drawn but it was possible to discern the layout of the suite. Carefully he studied it. It undoubtedly was a mirror image of the one where Exner and Reilly were staying. There was no place to hide. The only hope he had of getting to them would be to let himself into their suite in the middle of the night and use the surprise factor. It wouldn't be hard to take care of the old lady. It was Reilly who might be a problem.

He studied the sofa. It was obviously a convertible. This

would be where Reilly slept in the other suite. Even though she might be awake and hear him come in, with the element of surprise he could crack her head before she had time to call out or reach for the phone. From the sofa he ran back down to the foyer. Eight seconds. That was all the time he needed.

There was one problem. If blood spattered on either bed, no one would believe that the two women had disappeared because Reilly was trying to keep Exner from falling off the terrace.

A pillow. Over their faces. No trace that way. In the duskiness of the quiet penthouse Cameron Hardwick smiled. The slow-acting knockout drops that had served him so well at casinos would be useful again. They took a couple of hours to take effect completely. It wouldn't be that hard to slip them in Exner's drink at dinner, or else he'd manage to join her and Reilly for a nightcap in one of the lounges. It would be too much to drug them both. Reilly would get suspicious if they both started fading at once.

He had four nights to make it happen but the last night, Friday, would be the safest. In the confusion of docking early Saturday morning, they wouldn't be missed immediately.

The plan would work. He'd make sure it did. And next week he'd collect the two hundred thousand dollars that was just waiting for him in the safe deposit box.

Hardwick put his ear against the outside door of the suite and listened. He heard a faint buzzing sound, then the steward's voice. "Flowers for you, Lady Exner."

Hardwick opened the door a crack. As the steward's back disappeared into the opposite suite, he hurried down the corridor to the stairs and back to the anonymity of the public rooms.

Oxford

At headquarters in Oxford, Superintendent Livingston had been very glad to hear from Regan Reilly so soon. After he said good-bye to her, he hung up the phone, swirled his chair around so that it faced the window and leaned back, his favorite position when he was thinking. He approved of Regan's suggestion to obtain copies of the coverage of the death of Athena Popolous from her hometown newspapers. The Popolous family lawyer had made arrangements to have the body returned to Greece. Apparently the parents were in seclusion. Even though it had been more than ten years since they had seen their daughter, they had still always clung to the hope that one day she would return.

His review of the old file as well as his conversations with the lawyer made it obvious to him that the Popolous family was both affluent and influential. Undoubtedly the discovery of the missing girl's body would be major news in Athens and would receive extensive media coverage. Pushing back the irritation that acquiring the newspapers hadn't occurred to him first, Livingston again reached for the phone. When he left his office fifteen minutes later, it was with the assurance that copies of papers reporting the Popolous case could be translated and faxed to him and to Regan Reilly on the *Queen Guinevere*.

His first stop was a five-minute drive away, to the bedside of Penelope Atwater in Royal Oxford Hospital. He braced himself for the rather nasty sight of Penelope, as he had seen her last night, her face ashen, her lips cracked and dry, intravenous tubes attached to her roly-poly arms, a hospital shirt perilously close to revealing the unthinkable, all of this enveloped in a stinky haze that left no doubt as to the abominable condition of her innards.

After depositing his Renault in the carpark, Livingston gulped in a precious few breaths of fresh air, then resolutely pushed through the revolving door into the nearly empty lobby. The janitor mopping the tile floor was using a dark green cleaning solution that never failed to make Nigel's eyes itch and little bumps appear on his already razor-burned neck. He hurried to the clerk in charge of visitors' passes, who was wearing a red-and-white-striped uniform and a badge which proclaimed that to date she had volunteered ten thousand hours to Royal Oxford Hospital.

This is your life, Livingston thought as he asked for and received a pass to visit the ailing Penelope. Scratching his neck, he rushed to the lift. If I'd sat in that lobby for ten thousand hours, I'd have turned into a life-sized hive, he thought.

Penelope Atwater was in room 210. If possible, Livingston decided, she looked worse today than she had last evening. As he drew up a chair to the bed, he felt genuinely remorseful that he had to question her. When she breathed in his direction he also felt sorry for himself. He waited patiently as in response to his inquiry about how she felt, she flooded him with precise and unwanted information. "But," she croaked, "at least I'm alive, which is more than I can say for my sweet old roommate."

Livingston glanced at the stripped bed under the window. "I'd assumed she'd been discharged."

"In a manner of speaking," Penelope belched. "Oh, beg your pardon."

"Hmmm, yes, of course." Livingston turned to the business at hand. "Miss Atwater, I do hate to trouble you, but you seem so absolutely sure there was no possibility that you might have mistakenly included arsenic as an ingredient in your hors d'oeuvres."

"I call them my tasty pasties," she quavered.

"Quite so. Now if my notes are correct, you took the remaining . . . er . . . tasty pasties up to your room. That would suggest that since they all came from the same batch, if they had been completely eaten by the guests on either Saturday evening or Sunday afternoon, someone else would have gotten ill. The fact that only you became ill after bringing the leftovers to your room is rather odd."

Livingston pulled out his notebook and flipped the pages rapidly. "You did not feel particularly well Saturday night but recovered enough to enjoy more tasty pasties on Sunday afternoon as well as a normal dinner."

"Oh yes." Atwater's eyes brightened. "For Sunday dinner, after you and the young ladies left, Lady Exner and Val and Philip and I enjoyed some bangers and mash. You see, Saturday night I had really just a touch of normal distress which accompanies a delicate constitution. Sunday night was entirely different. It wasn't until I went up to my room and treated myself to the last of the tasty pasties on my bedside table that I became violently ill."

Livingston looked up sharply. "I understood that you brought the remaining tasty pasties up with you when you retired Sunday evening. Are you saying that you had left them in your room earlier?"

Penelope looked guilty. "You see, they go over so well and I was afraid the girls would eat them all up, so, when I excused myself for a moment, I slipped six or seven of them in a napkin and took them to my room."

"So they were in your room for anyone to see most of the afternoon and evening?"

Finally Penelope seemed to understand the drift of the questioning. Her eyes widened. Her mouth formed a circle. Her chubby hands clasped the hospital shirt. "You mean someone might have sprinkled arsenic on them while they were in my room? But who? And why?"

Livingston stood up. He patted her shoulder. "That's what I intend to find out."

* * *

As he left the hospital grounds Livingston made a quick decision. A right turn would have started him toward Llewellyn Hall. A left turn led to the main street of Oxford and the Kings Arms Pub. He chose the latter, deciding that a quick sandwich and a cup of tea would be very welcome before he met Philip Whitcomb, his fiancée, Val Twyler, and the maid for further questioning. Philip had assured them that they would be at the Hall all day.

It was still early for lunch and the pub was nearly empty. Livingston ordered a cheese-and-tomato sandwich and a pot of tea. The waiter had just served him when the front door opened and he heard his name being called. Claire James hurried to his table.

"Hi there, Inspectah. What a surprise to see you here. Oh, you're havin' just what I was fixin' to order. May I join you?" She did not quite wait for his nod of assent as she slipped into the seat opposite him.

Livingston had been hoping for a quiet lunch with a chance to think, but on the other hand, he decided, this young woman had been here at college with Athena Popolous, and a chance to talk with her one-on-one just might prove to be fruitful. He certainly could use even a glimmer of new information, and besides, he admitted to himself, Claire James was very attractive in her spandex bicycling outfit.

As she signaled for the waiter, Claire explained that she was staying in Oxford for an extra couple of days after the reunion. "It gets kind of borin' after everybody else is gone, but my fiancé is meetin' me here tomorrow and then we're headin' up to Scotland. I just love to travel."

The waiter arrived. "I'll have just what this handsome man here is havin'," she said, smiling coyly at Livingston. That settled, Claire leaned forward, her attitude became conspiratorial, her voice dropped to a near whisper. "Have you discovered yet who strangled poor old Athena?"

Livingston tried not to sound annoyed. "The investigation is continuing."

"Well, I just bet the trail is mighty cold after ten years. Who knows, her killer could be dead by now." Claire widened her eyes, seeming to enjoy the possibility.

Livingston took a savage bite of the sandwich he had wanted to savor.

"And I heard about poor Penelope. When I saw her stuff all those crackers in a napkin, I just knew she was going to get sick."

Livingston's eyes narrowed. "You saw her?"

"Who could have missed her? She left a path of crumbs Hansel and Gretel would have envied."

Livingston remembered that Hansel and Gretel had been lost in the forest because the birds had eaten those crumbs. What bird or vulture had followed Penelope's crumbs?

Livingston chose his next words carefully. Trying to sound offhand, he said, "Miss James, the other day you mentioned again that you thought Athena Popolous had a romantic interest in Professor Philip Whitcomb. Of course he vehemently denied it and I noticed the other young ladies didn't seem to agree with you. What was the basis for your hunch?"

"It's not just a hunch. When I was out bicyclin' today I remembered bicyclin' with Athena. Just the Sunday before she disappeared Athena and I went bicyclin' and ended up ridin' past Llewellyn Hall. As usual Philip was out messin' around with his flowers. Even though he has his own apartment at school, everyone knew that weekends you could always find him there. Athena stopped by to say hello. When I teased her later that she went down that road on purpose she just turned all beet-red. I just had that feelin' that somethin' was goin' on between those two, and thinkin' back, he wasn't surprised to see her."

"Didn't it occur to you to mention this ten years ago?"

"Heavens no. Everyone thought Athena had just taken off on her own and Philip certainly hadn't. He was still here, workin' away in the garden. But now that they found her body on the property next to Llewellyn Hall, it makes you wonder, doesn't it?

It certainly does, Livingston thought as he called for the check. Despite her halfhearted protest, he paid for Claire's lunch. He decided that she had certainly earned her cheese-and-tomato sandwich.

As he approached Llewellyn Hall, Livingston drove slowly, envisioning Athena Popolous riding down this quiet country lane on her bicycle hoping to catch a glimpse of Philip Whitcomb. For the life of him, he could never fathom the taste of teenagers. In his wildest dreams he could not imagine his fifteen-year-old daughter Davina having a crush on the likes of Philip. "Gross me out," she'd say, her lip curled. But, he admitted to himself, even Philip would be a vast improvement over the prehistoric-looking creatures, so-called rock stars, whose likenesses immortalized on posters graced every inch of wall space in Davina's room.

Athena Popolous had been last seen in the Bull and Bear pub near the train station. No witness had been able to say whether she was on the train, which of course did not prove she hadn't been on board. On Friday nights dozens of Oxford students leave for London. They now knew that even if she had intended to take the train, the probability was that something had happened between the pub and the station.

The gate to the Exner estate was open. Livingston turned into the oval driveway and parked in front of the manor house. He felt his senses quickening as he rang the bell. Nearly forty-eight hours ago he had come here to interrogate the classmates of the murdered Athena Popolous. Lady Exner's companion, Penelope Atwater, had not known Athena Popolous, but around the time of his visit an attempt had been made to poison her. Why? Was there a connection between the two crimes and, if so, what could it possibly be?

The maid answered the door. Livingston remembered her name as he stepped into the foyer. Emma Horne. Rapidly he reviewed the information he had taken from her on Saturday. She worked afternoons at Llewellyn Hall and had done so for the past dozen years. Her aunt had been Sir Gilbert's housekeeper and later stayed on with Lady Exner until her retirement. That was when Emma Horne had taken over. Studying the woman's bone-thin face, Livingston detected a trace of wry humor in her expression. He decided that before he left, a trip to the kitchen for a chat with her would be in order.

At his inquiry, Emma told him that Professor Whitcomb and Miss Twyler were on the back porch and were expecting him.

The porch, like everything in the house, was in need of painting. The furniture consisted of an aging glider and matching rockers with a rickety round glass table cluttered with stacks of newspapers. Val Twyler was leaning back in the glider, one pointed toe pushing on the floor causing it to sway uncertainly. She was wearing a khaki skirt and matching blouse, which somehow made Livingston think of a prim Girl Guide. Another organization his daughter refused to join. Her smile when she greeted him was polite rather than warm.

On the other hand, Philip Whitcomb was visibly distressed. His sandy hair had a disheveled look, as though he had forgotten to comb it that morning. The knees of his light blue cotton trousers had traces of dirt, suggesting that he had been gardening. With his tongue he kept moistening the lips of his even-featured bland face.

"I say, Inspector, I'm appalled."

Livingston waited.

"Penelope rang from hospital after you left her. Surely the laboratory is mistaken. You can't seriously believe that someone tried to poison that woman. She's constantly experiencing stomach ailments."

"Not of this magnitude," Livingston said quietly.

"But for what possible reason?" Twyler's voice sounded disdainful. "It simply doesn't make sense."

"Apparently not," Livingston agreed, "which is why, if there is a simple answer, I'd like to find it. Since no one else became ill after eating the . . ." He hesitated.

"Tasty pasties," Philip said helpfully.

"Exactly. I certainly agree that Miss Atwater might have inadvertently added the wrong ingredient when she was preparing the treats, but since no one else became ill it does suggest that the poisonous ingredient was added after she brought some six or seven of them to her room as a nighttime snack. I wonder if I may look over her room."

It seemed to Livingston that Philip's expression changed from distress to annoyance. "I thought the search your people made last evening was very thorough."

"Professor Whitcomb, when we get a report from hospital that poison was found in a patient's system, we must investigate most thoroughly. The laboratory confirmed this morning that the crackers found in her bed contain traces of arsenic. Now, if you don't mind, I'd like to have a look for myself."

"Of course, of c-c-c-course." Philip opened the door and called for Emma.

It was a bit of luck, Livingston decided, that neither Whitcomb nor Twyler chose to accompany him. He climbed the winding staircase to the second floor, puffing a bit at the effort. He observed that the aging carpet was threadbare and sections of the wallpaper in the spacious hallway were completely missing. "A proper mess this house has become," Emma Horne said reprovingly. "Herself has wanted to keep it the way it was when Sir Gilbert was alive, and Philip is just as bad. He doesn't notice that it's falling down around him."

At the top of the staircase she led the way to the right. "All the bedrooms they use are in this wing," Horne announced. "Lady Exner's is the first, then Philip's, a guest room after that, and the end one is Penelope's. The door past that is the W.C."

"The W.C.!" Livingston exclaimed. "Doesn't Lady Exner have a private bath?"

"No," Emma said shortly as she led the way to Penelope's

room. "Anyone else would have converted one of these huge closets or maybe a guest room into a bath, but what was good enough for Sir Gilbert is good enough for her. Doesn't really matter. She and Penelope share. There are two loos in the other wing and two on the main floor, but at present this is the only working one. Her Ladyship's finally arranged to have the plumbing repair started, but it will be several months before the new fixtures are delivered."

They were at the door of Penelope's bedroom. The bed had been remade. The luggage Penelope had planned to take on the trip was stacked in a corner. The top of the dresser was littered with odds and ends, making Livingston think of an abandoned gift shop. Scattered around the room were teddy bears of various shapes and sizes. The bed and the night table beside it were in full view from the entrance.

Livingston stepped back into the foyer. "Are you saying that anyone who desired to use the W.C. on Sunday afternoon had to come up to this one?" He pointed to the lavatory to the right of Penelope's room.

"Yes, sir. Ridiculous, isn't it? You must know how valuable this property is. A hotel chain has been after Lady Exner to sell even half of it. A fortune she could make, then she could do this place properly and enjoy it. Philip's just as bad. Him and his garden! I must say, however, he seems to be getting a little more aware of creature comforts as he gets older."

"Quite so." Livingston retraced his steps and walked down the foyer again as though he were headed for the W.C. He realized that at the sight of an open door most people instinctively glanced into a room. That meant that anyone here on Sunday who chose to use the facilities could have seen the purloined tasty pasties at Penelope's bedside. He inspected the room and returned downstairs, realizing he had established opportunity but certainly not motive.

When Livingston rejoined Twyler and Whitcomb on the terrace, it was clear to him that they had been quarreling. Philip Whitcomb's normally pale face was flushed. His forehead was furrowed, accentuating his seemingly permanent expression of a bewildered scholar. Except, Livingston thought, he's now a very angry bewildered scholar, or else is giving an excellent imitation of one. Livingston realized he did not know why that thought had risen unbidden from his subconscious.

Valerie Twyler did not seem to be angry so much as forceful. She was leaning forward in her seat, her hands clasped, her eyes fixed unwaveringly onto Whitcomb's face. She did not seem to notice Livingston's return as she said, "Philip, my dear, I know how distasteful and horrible this is for you, but you simply must admit that it is a distinct possibility, and rather than have Livingston looking for a potential murderer, we must stop this nonsense in its tracks."

"But Val, I s-s-say, it's so disloyal."

Was it really possible that neither one of them heard my footsteps? Livingston thought. He wondered if this exchange was for his benefit. But then maybe not. "I'm afraid I should have a heavier step," he said as they both looked up, their expressions now startled. "I could not help overhearing what you said just now and I most urgently suggest that if there is anything you know that can shed some light on this investigation, it is your duty to share it with me."

"Philip." Twyler's hand reached over and patted his shoulder.

"Oh, g-g-go ahead if you must, but, Inspector"—Philip stood up and shoved his hands in his pockets—"this m-m-must be confidential. I mean you certainly wouldn't press charges on an ei-ei-eighty-year-old woman, would you?"

"An eighty-year-old woman?" Livingston could not keep the astonishment from his voice.

"Mmmmm." Philip shook his head. "Of course to her it was a prank, a . . . I-I-I don't know."

"Philip, allow me." Val turned to Livingston. "Inspector, how much arsenic was found on those tasty pasties and how much in Penelope's body?"

"A trace," Livingston said. "Very little, actually."

"Certainly not enough to intentionally kill her."

"Intentionally—difficult to say. You must remember, Miss Atwater is an overweight woman who has not taken very good care of herself. She has digestive problems, high blood pressure, an overworked heart, a very high cholesterol count. She could easily have had a heart attack from the extreme distress she was in, and in that case whoever added arsenic to the tasty pasties could have been guilty of murder. Fortunately for that person, she is going to recover. Now what did you want to tell me?"

"Veronica—Lady Exner—very much wanted to take this trip without Penelope. To be honest, Penelope has been getting on her nerves lately. They've traveled together a great deal recently, and while in some ways the companionship was welcomed, in others it had begun to grate. As Penelope gets older she eats more. Actually she's put on two stone in the last ten months. Veronica has said she sometimes thinks they should name a food processor after her.

"Last week Veronica was out in the potting shed with Philip. He has a jar of arsenic, clearly labeled, and Veronica commented that the next time Penelope made tasty pasties he might want to try mixing a trace of arsenic in them. That way, when she spent the night running to the loo and interminably flushing the toilet, at least she'd have a reason to be sick."

"Surely you're not suggesting—"

"That she acted on her own witticism," Philip broke in. "Val, I told you that as a j-j-joke. Veronica wasn't serious."

"I know she wasn't serious then, but Sunday morning when Penelope went to church service, Veronica said that she was sure her niece would find it terribly difficult to have Penelope on her hands for a month. She again brought up sending Penelope off on her own holiday and going alone to the States. Philip wouldn't hear of it. Then, when Penelope had to be rushed to hospital, Veronica said something about how sorry she was but doesn't life always have a silver lining to go with every cloud. Now she'd get her wish to travel sans Penelope and not hurt her feelings."

"Only you substituted Regan Reilly as a companion," Livingston commented.

"Yes," Philip said. "Actually my aunt didn't m-m-mind that at all. She thinks Regan is quite fun, and of course when she gets to the States her cousin will take over. I warned Regan that Veronica is very unpredictable and she must w-w-watch her as one would a child."

"But you see, Veronica got her way," Val pointed out.

"Yes, I see that." Livingston walked to the railing of the porch and looked out over the formal country garden. Amazing, the amount of work that must go into those exquisitely laid-out beds. Frankly, gardening bored the hell out of him. "A labor of love, clearly," Livingston commented.

"We have three blooms a year," Philip said, coming to stand beside Livingston. "A great joy to work with one's hands, to feel the earth in your f-f-fingers, to see seedlings sprout."

Livingston glanced at him, then followed Philip Whitcomb's gaze. He was not looking at the beds of flowers but over them to the left, where the woods began and from where there were faint sounds of construction. It was there that the skeletal remains of Athena Popolous had been uncovered.

Philip, seeming to sense Livingston's calculating stare, turned restlessly. "I want a cup of tea," he declared. "Inspector?"

It was not the most gracious invitation Livingston had ever received, but he quickly accepted and just as quickly noted the annoyed expression on Whitcomb's face.

"I'll ask Emma to pour it." Val got up from the glider. Clearly she shared Philip's resentment at Livingston's continued presence.

When she left the porch, Livingston said, "Professor Whitcomb, there is something I must ask you and I prefer to do it in Miss Twyler's absence. It has again been suggested that Athena Popolous had a schoolgirl attachment to you. I must ask you to be entirely frank with me. Did she ever in any way pursue you, perhaps try to use you as a confidant?"

Philip's face flushed. "A-a-absolutely not. I simply would-would-wouldn't have any part of her."

"Then she did try to single you out," Livingston said swiftly.

"She-she-she got in the habit of pedaling past here on Su-Su-Sunday afternoons when I was in the front gardens. It was most a-a-annoying."

"How frequently did she pedal by and how often did she stop?"

"Several times. I tried to get r-r-rid of her immediately. I was sorry for her. She was so ob-obviously unhappy. I should have been stern with her."

"Professor, please understand. My questions are simply directed to learning whether Athena Popolous may have confided or tried to confide in you about an unhappy love affair or any problem that might help lead us to her killer."

Philip bit his lip nervously. "Whenever she ma-ma-managed to corner me, it was to say she couldn't g-get over her aunt's death. Naturally it was difficult not to listen to her. I told her she should g-get more involved with the other students . . . make friends she could confide in. When I stressed it was in-in-inappropriate to visit me outside Saint Polycarp's, she simply showed up anyway. That ha-happened off and on five or six times when I was working in the front garden on Sunday afternoons."

"Then the last time you saw her was . . ."

"The Sunday before she dis-disappeared."

"Why didn't you simply tell me this on Saturday when Claire James said Athena had an attachment to you?"

"Because I didn't h-have an attachment to her and it was m-most embarrassing."

"I'm afraid embarrassment is not the issue in a murder case. Professor, if you can try to remember even one of your conversations with Athena Popolous in which she mentioned a name or plans she may have had, I'd be most grateful. Ah, here is Miss Twyler and Miss Horne with the tea. I'm afraid I really can't stay after all."

Livingston gave his regrets to Val, aware that apologies were totally unnecessary. In the car he hesitated at the end of the driveway as he weighed his options. He was anxious to see if the lab had any further results of forensic tests performed on Athena's body. He also wanted to pay a visit to the headmaster of St. Polycarp's.

The headmaster won.

Livingston had always felt that Reginald Crane was a man supremely equipped for his job. St. Polycarp's, after all, was a one-year or even one-term school. Students came and went, some soaking in the cultural experience of studying in the Oxford community. Others, like Athena Popolous, were sent there under protest and never participated in the town life around them. Reginald Crane was aware of the student jokes about the narrow beds, threadbare blankets, and antiquated furniture. He serenely dismissed the complaints. "Toughen up the spoiled kids," he had once confided to Livingston. "Budget's small enough. I'd rather spend it on offering them a wider variety of courses."

A different man might have chafed under the endless change in the student body and the impossibility of creating any real esprit de corps such as a four-year college engendered. And yet many former students did show up for their ten-year reunion, however informal it really was. When they came they still joked about the facilities yet seemed to be aware that their stay at St. Polycarp's had been, after all, a broadening experience. Crane had managed to gather together a superior staff of teachers, despite the relatively low pay.

Livingston was ushered into Crane's private office, a wood-paneled room covered with bookshelves whose volumes testified to the scholarly mind of the headmaster. In his early sixties, Crane looked like a human thermometer, with his pencil-thin body, ruddy complexion and generous head of silver hair.

Livingston apologized for the intrusion. "Don't like to simply burst in," he explained as he sat down in a reasonably comfortable chair near Crane's desk. In Livingston's eight years in Oxford, he and Crane had become close friends.

"You never burst in, Nigel," Crane told him, "you come without phoning because you're dealing with something that can't be put off." He leaned back in his wide leather chair and folded his long sinewy hands. "As my American students would say, 'What's up?' "

Livingston decided to get to the point without preamble. "I want your honest, absolutely confidential opinion of Philip Whitcomb."

Crane shrugged. "Absolutely confidential?"

"Of course."

"Then I have to say," Crane hesitated, "that it's hard to say. A good, even very good teacher. Knows his subject. Loves it. The man is transformed when he discusses or reads poetry. Almost a visionary aura about him. Too much, for my taste. After all, the poets were mere mortals. I doubt they read their own poetry with all the histrionics Philip manages to contrive. But I do know he's made students whose idea of poetry was of the 'Roses are red, Violets are blue' category begin to understand the concept of what makes a poem a classic. For that I am grateful, and students ought to be so.

"On the other hand, outside the classroom I find him quite dull. Can't speak without blushing or stuttering, all wrapped up in his flower garden . . . I'm sure he'd rather plant flowers than eat. How he managed to get engaged to be married I'll never know. I suspect Valerie did all the courting, not the other way around."

"My impression exactly." Livingston weighed his next question, then asked it carefully. "If Philip is so persuasive in class, does he have any problems with students falling in love with him?"

Crane's face darkened. "Not anymore."

"Not anymore?" Livingston pounced on the words. "What do you mean?"

The headmaster obviously wished he had not been so blunt. "Perhaps I'm being unfair. After all, it was a long time ago. Eleven years, as a matter of fact. Philip was still quite young then, in his early thirties, I should think. A student started following him around like a puppy. He was flattered, I gather, and spent private time with her—something absolutely forbidden. There must be no individual relationships between students and teachers at Saint Polycarp's. Apparently Philip tired of the girl and started avoiding her. You can imagine how I felt when she burst into my office and announced she was carrying his baby."

Livingston let out a soundless whistle. "Was she?"

"No. She was a highly emotional, even hysterical girl. Fortunately for us, she had made the same accusations about a teacher at a previous school. It wasn't hard to get the truth from her. Her relationship with Philip had been confined to some bike riding and picnics. Even so, it could have been a scandal, even a disaster, for the school, if she had persisted in her accusations. I came within an inch of sacking Philip, but he pleaded for his job. You must realize this position suits him exactly. He's teaching a subject he loves, he has acres and acres of property to garden and he's obviously Lady Exner's heir."

"I would suppose he is," Livingston agreed.

"I warned him most strongly that if even a hint of involvement with a student occurred again, he was out, and with a highly prejudicial reference."

"I see. You're quite sure that was eleven years ago."

"Very sure. I remember exactly because it was the year before the Popolous girl disappeared. At the time of all the unfortunate publicity about the 'Greek girl who never returned to class,' I kept thinking how it would have been the end of Saint Polycarp's if one year before a student had become pregnant by a teacher or even persisted in her claim that she was. As it is, I've been called several times this week by local papers asking for my comments on the discovery of Athena Popolous's body." The headmaster turned penetrating eyes on Livingston. "I realize you can't disclose why you've asked about Philip, but I hope you understand that I'm responsible for five hundred students. Perhaps you should consider whether it is my responsibility to know what is going on."

Livingston did not hesitate. There was no question Headmaster Crane had residual anger, even contempt, for Philip for the scandal he could have caused St. Polycarp's. Without proof it was unfair even to suggest that he might have had any kind of relationship with Athena Popolous. "For the moment we are simply doing routine questioning."

The headmaster's sardonic expression told Livingston that routine questioning was a feeble cover for a purposeful investigation. For the second time that afternoon, Livingston left a meeting with the distinct impression that his absence was more honored than his presence.

At headquarters Livingston was informed that there were further developments in the Popolous case. The pockets of Athena's jacket had been lined with plastic. One of them had a hole on the inside. The forensic staff had found a matchbook from the Bull and Bear that had fallen through the hole, jammed deep into the lining of her coat. It had been well preserved. Scrawled inside the matchbook were two letters—B.A.—and three numbers—315.

He went into his private office, settled at his desk, and wearily rubbed his head. Athena Popolous had been in the Bull and Bear on the night she disappeared. Did she write in the matchbook that night, or had it been in her pocket for months? Were the letters someone's initials and a meeting time? Was it part of a license plate?

Somehow Livingston felt that this information was related to her disappearance and death.

At Sea

VERONICA SCOOPED UP the Daily Program from the dresser and sat down on her bed. "Regan, we must hurry and decide what activities we will join today. It's five before eleven, and there are several here that start at eleven o'clock."

"What are the choices, Veronica?" Regan asked as she thought longingly of relaxing downstairs in a deck chair by the pool, reading a book and observing the activities of her fellow inhabitants of this microcosm known as the *Queen Guinevere*.

"Well, let's see. There's a bridge lecture which doesn't interest me, a computer lecture which would do me no good . . . how to detect the early stages of plantar's warts as taught by a podiatrist . . . certainly not before lunch. Aha! Here we go. A financial planning seminar about the different styles of money management. As Sir Gilbert used to say, money can't buy you happiness, but at least it pays for everything else." Veronica laughed and jumped up, reaching for her hair spray.

"I really don't know that much about money matters. Philip has hired an accountant for me who balances my checkbook. But it's high time I learned a bit more. Besides, this is probably one of the few lectures that will attract more men than women."

"The truth comes out, Veronica," Regan teased as she opened the terrace door and squinted at the brilliant sunlight.

"Ah, yes, well . . . afterward we can have lunch out on the Lido Deck and then proceed to the psychic's session," Veronica continued. "I've had my chart done several times by various astrologers and I always welcome a new voice to predict my future. And then of course there's a bingo game at four-thirty in the Knights Lounge.

Having every minute accounted for reminded Regan of Girl Scout camp. Twenty years ago she and her buddy Sally had been admonished by their Scout leader for taking longer than the schedule permitted to collect kindling wood for the campfire stew. And when they returned to civilization Luke and Nora were pulled aside at the bus stop by the disgruntled troop leader who informed them of Regan's poor twig-gathering skills, which threw off the schedule of all the girls and left no time to bug bomb the latrines before dark. And to think that Regan was one of the two in the troop who could boast record-setting sales of Girl Scout cookies. The other one was a pint-sized nudge who insisted it was unfair that Regan sell them to people who came to the funeral parlor for wakes. Regan had just gotten lucky that one of the ancient Sheas had died the week of the sale.

Down in the boardroom about a dozen people had gathered for the financial seminar and more were wandering in. As Veronica led the way to the front of the room, Luke turned around and gave Regan a quick wink.

"I think that nice-looking man is flirting with you," Veronica whispered.

She doesn't miss a thing, Regan thought as they grabbed two places in the front row. Luke was two seats behind and Regan could feel him smirking. Okay, Dad. Just you wait. You'll see.

Hand in hand, Mario and Immaculata entered the forward door of the boardroom and waved a hello.

"So you're here to figure how to spend your travelers' checks too, huh?" Mario chuckled. "The missus and I won a few bucks in the casino last night and we thought we'd learn how to manage it."

"All three dollars that's left of it," Immaculata beamed as she held up a shopping bag. "Mario bought me some new clothes upstairs in the promenade. I wanted to buy a few things for Concepcione and Mario the Third, but big Mario said no way, he wanted to spend it all on me."

"Could everyone please take a seat?" A bespectacled young man with blond hair and a somber Brooks Brothers suit started to distribute folders to everyone as he introduced himself. "My name is Norman Bennett and I am a financial consultant and portfolio manager. I'll be spending the next few days with you helping you set up your investment objectives."

Veronica leaned over and with a stage whisper that could have been heard deep in the engine room declared, "He's rather handsome, Regan. Maybe he's available."

Mortified, Regan looked down and leafed through the questionnaire inside the folder. I don't really know what I think about the state of the United States economy in the long run. It's enough of a challenge to get my own taxes done. What would I do if I inherited a million dollars today? I'd hire a seaplane to come get me.

She glanced around the room to see which other passengers had come to learn financial wizardry. A sprinkling of young couples, honeymoon types, were scattered through the audience. But Veronica was right. Of the two dozen or so in the room, at least three quarters were men. Again, Regan made eye contact with Luke. He smiled and discreetly pointed to Norman Bennett. Clearly he had overheard Veronica sizing up the financial guru.

Veronica hissed, "Regan dear, Mr. Bennett is about to begin. Do pay attention."

I can't wait, Regan thought, as she caught Cameron Hardwick coming in and settling himself in the last row. He must be checking out the competition, she decided as Norman Bennett cleared his throat.

"The setting of investment objectives for a substantial pool of assets is not only important, but vital. Yes, vital. However, it has historically been vastly complicated by misunderstandings due to . . ."

Oh my God, Regan thought.

A half hour later, as the droning continued with only brief respites to draw graphs on the blackboard, Veronica was still perched on the edge of her seat, shaking her head in passionate agreement with all of Norman Bennett's points of light. Regan was fighting to blink the sleep from her eyes and keep an interested look on her face.

"And now for our question-and-answer period. Please feel free to pick my brains." Bennett's lips pursed and curved upward in a muscular convulsion, an expression that brought Gomer Pyle to mind.

No questions, please, please, Regan prayed, tapping her feet on the carpeted floor of the boardroom.

Veronica leapt from her seat.

"Mr. Bennett, you have been discussing the attractive return of twenty-year bonds. In your opinion, would they be a sound investment for one of my uncertain years?"

Regan heard a giggle from one of the honeymooners and turned around to glare.

Bennett cleared his throat yet again. "There are so many wonderful areas in which to invest that I would prefer to have you complete the questionnaire and return it before we go into specifics."

Score one for Bennett, Regan thought.

The next question came from Mario Buttacavola. "You made some interesting points about the possibilities for investing in Eastern Europe. I heard something about a big Russian truck company that wants foreign capital. Do you think that's safe?" He did not give Bennett a chance to answer. "Say, I've got a good idea," he boomed. "There's someone here, Cameron Hardwick, who sits at our table, and he's a big financial expert. Maybe both of you could give us your opinions. That would be real interesting."

"You are, of course, referring to the Boris and Vanya trucking company, which is following the example of its biggest competitor by offering to sell forty-nine percent of its stock to foreign investors. I'd be very interested to hear what Mr. Hardwick has to say about this." Bennett sounded genuinely enthusiastic.

Mario was obviously pleased to have the floor. "Well, Cameron just came back from checking out the Eastern European countries for investment possibilities for his private clients. What do you say, Cameron?" he asked, turning to the back of the room.

All heads turned their gaze on Hardwick. He remained in his seat and waved away the question. "I'd rather hear what you have to say about it."

Mario said persuasively, "Oh, come on, Cameron. We're not asking you to talk about your clients. Let me put it this way. Would you consider this a good buy generally?"

Hardwick stood up and gripped the chair in front of him. "I deal with my clients one-on-one. I think that Mr. Bennett is the one you came to hear." Clearly he was forcing a smile. "Now if you'll excuse me." He strode from the room.

Bennett broke the uneasy silence that followed. "It has been my experience that most of my financial colleagues enjoy putting forth their views. However, we must respect Mr. Hardwick's wish not to do so. Now in my opinion . . ."

Ten minutes later, as they were leaving the boardroom, Mario and Immaculata joined Regan and Lady Exner. "Is that Hardwick guy some kind of stiff or what?" Mario asked. "You want to know something—I'll bet dollars to doughnuts he never heard of that company. In my book that guy is either dumb or a phony."

SYLVIE WANDERED THROUGH the Astolat Lounge, the Knights Lounge and the Lancelot Bar before she located Milton Wanamaker and his ever-present sister, Violet Cohn, sipping a Bloody Mary in the glassed-in section of the Lido Deck. On her third casual glance around the room she managed to meet Milton's eye. With a dazzling smile she made a beeline for his table.

"Enjoying our beautiful weather today?" she asked as she placed one hand on the empty chair between Milton and his sister.

"The patch behind my ear fell off last night and I woke up feeling queasy. There's nothing worse than motion sickness. I still haven't gotten my sea legs and I'm not feeling myself," Violet complained.

That could only be an improvement, Sylvie thought as Milton quickly rose to his feet.

"Please join us for a drink." With one hand he pulled out the chair for her, with the other he signaled for the waiter. "What would you like, Sylvie?"

"Same as you. I'd love a Bloody Mary."

"Ours is nonalcoholic," Violet announced, her tone and expression clearly disapproving.

"That's known as a Bloody Shame," Sylvie said airily.

"I agree," Milton said heartily. When the waiter came he ordered two Bloodys. He looked at his sister. "Violet?"

"I just want plain tomato juice. This has much too many spices. The patch fell off my ear last night—"

Sylvie noticed the look of resignation on Milton's face as he interrupted, "And we'll also have a plain tomato juice."

Last night Milton had asked her to dance while his sister was in the ladies' room. Now as Sylvie crossed her legs, she quietly noted his lean frame under the expensive sports shirt, the blue eyes, intelligent with a slight twinkle, and the well-barbered white hair that framed the bald dome he made no effort to conceal, thank God. Sylvie had met too many of the type who grow hair long on the sides and then, in an attempt to defy gravity, comb it back up and over their scalp, plastering it into place. She silently prayed Milton wasn't planning to attend the hair-replacement seminar this afternoon. She now caught his frankly admiring gaze.

He likes me, she thought, and I like him. Don't blow it, she warned herself.

Last night when they had danced to "Satin Doll," they had hardly spoken. Sylvie had enjoyed the rare pleasure of dancing with an attractive man who didn't have two left feet. She had intuitively known that Milton Wanamaker was not someone who wanted a woman chattering in his ear over the music. They had just sat down at his table adjacent to the dance floor and exchanged primary information, the fact that she was from Palm Springs and a widow, that he was from Beverly Hills and a widower, when his sister Violet, whom he had just identified as a Miami resident, emerged from the powder room.

"I think I'm having a reaction to the patch, Milton," she had informed him, virtually ignoring Sylvie. "The warning says that it may cause dizziness and blurred vision. I believe I'm experiencing that. Will you please take me back to my stateroom?"

That had been the end of her romantic foray last night. Sylvie had seen it before. Sisters who were self-appointed watchdogs for their eligible brothers. Even after she had married Harold, Sylvie had never been able to break the ice between her and his sister Goldie. A sister-in-law could be far worse than any mother-in-law. And tended to be around forever.

Last night Violet had complained because the patch didn't work. This morning she's complaining because it fell off. Eyeing Violet with a manufactured look of sympathy on her face, Sylvie sized her up quickly. Early seventies, a good ten years older than her brother, with an expensive gray-and-white cotton dress that fell in a precise line from shoulder to mid-calf. It looks like a cover for an ironing board, Sylvie thought, and immediately proceeded to admire it. You're not going to squeeze me out, toots, she exulted as for a fleeting moment Violet visibly thawed.

"Gray is my favorite color," she acknowledged, then pointed in the direction of the bar. "That young man looks familiar. I'm sure we have met him somewhere."

Sylvie and Milton turned to follow her outstretched index finger. Cameron Hardwick was the object of Violet's attention.

Terrific, Sylvie thought. Let him keep her busy. Jumping up, she waved vigorously to Cameron, beckoning him to the table. He picked up his drink and began to cross the deck toward them.

Sylvie explained, "Cameron is seated at our table."

"I don't remember him, Violet," Milton said.

When Hardwick reached them, Sylvie swiftly began introductions. "And Mrs. Cohn is sure she knows you from somewhere."

Violet was staring at him with the intensity of a hawk about to descend on its prey. "I never forget a face. They used to say Herbert Hoover could kiss a baby when it was fourteen months old and recognize it twenty years later when it was eligible to vote. As my brother will verify, I have that same talent."

And I'll bet she never forgets a grudge either, Sylvie thought.

Violet narrowed her eyes. "It was ten or twelve years ago. Which trip? Oh, I know. Milton, remember when we went to Greece?" She turned to Sylvie. "It was eleven years ago. My dear husband Bruce had just died." Her face brightened. To Sylvie her smile was a triumphant snarl. "You were working in the Olympic Hotel as a waiter."

Hardwick's face darkened to crimson, then purple. "I've

never been to Greece. I think you ought to have that memory of yours checked."

He turned on his heel as Milton Wanamaker jumped up. "See here," Milton protested.

Sylvie put a restraining hand on his arm. "I'm so sorry I asked him over. I had no idea—"

Violet looked intensely satisfied. "Obviously he doesn't like to be reminded he was a waiter. He's probably insinuating he was born to the purple. Milton, remember how Sir John and Lady Victoria joked about the dreadful people who brag about fine connections?"

Sylvie saw the pride with which Violet dropped the names of her titled friends. Inspiration struck her. "It just occurred to me . . ." She hesitated. Should she call the battle axe Violet or Mrs. Cohn? Violet. We're going to see a lot of each other. ". . . I mean, I was just thinking, Violet, that you'd very much enjoy meeting Lady Exner, who also sits at my table. We've become very friendly and she's already suggested that I visit her estate in Oxford. It's called . . ." Oh, hell, what's it called? Sylvie thought frantically. Lolly? Louie? Lew . . . Lew . . . "Llewellyn Hall!"

Violet joyously agreed that a drink with Lady Exner during the Captain's Cocktail Party tonight would be a great pleasure. Then, sighing, she said her stomach was really pitching with the way the ship was rocking, and would dear Milton escort her to her cabin for a brief lie-down before luncheon?

Why don't you just get on your broom and fly back? Sylvie thought.

LADY EXNER AND Regan had lunch served on the private deck of the suite. As Regan pointed out, "Veronica, you've done the Sit-and-Be-Fit class; you've had a boat drill; you've attended a financial lecture, and it's just past noon. Why don't we order salads and relax for a couple of hours?"

"An excellent idea," Veronica agreed merrily. "The psychic session is at two-thirty, and before one consults with a psychic, one should meditate. Get in touch with one's inner life, deepest feelings, profound, unvoiced emotions."

There's nothing unvoiced in your life, Regan thought as she reached for the room-service menu. "How does chicken salad sound?"

"Delightful. Perfect for this balmy, sun-filled day. And don't forget a bottle of Dom Perignon."

"I just hope Philip and your accountant don't think the Dom Perignon is my idea," Regan commented.

"It's absolutely none of their business whether I drink dishwater or Dom Perignon," Veronica replied. "Besides, I foot the bill for acres of flowers every year that do not survive the winter chill."

She's more worldly than I realized, Regan thought with a grin. "No flies on you, Veronica."

"Such a quaint American expression, and you're absolutely right."

The champagne did the double duty of keeping Veronica's spirits joyous throughout lunch and then putting her to sleep in the chaise longue on the deck as soon as she laid down her fork. Regan sipped her second glass as she stared out at the horizon.

The soft peal of the telephone did not disturb Veronica's mercifully even breathing. Regan hurried to answer it. Who would possibly be calling? Surely not Luke or Nora. Livingston? "Hello." Regan realized she sounded nervous.

A crackling sound filled her ear. "Hold on, please, from New York." Do operators purposely sound like Lily Tomlin? Regan wondered.

"Regan," a voice boomed. "How was the reunion? I hear Athena put in an appearance."

"JEFF." Regan laughed reluctantly. "I gather Kit filled you in."

"I talked to her last night. I had called New Jersey expecting to find you keening for your father's clients at Reilly's Remains." His tone changed, became solicitous. "How are you doing? From what Kit tells me, you've taken on quite a job."

Veronica's breathing was changing to a short-long-short wheeze. Through the open door to the sun deck, Regan eyed her apprehensively. "For one thing, I'm sitting here drinking Dom Perignon."

"Save some for me."

"Too late. The bottle's upside down in the ice bucket. What are you doing in New York?"

"I'm here for a couple of weeks working on a film."

"Oh, anything good?" Regan asked.

"It's an action film. I play a terrorist who turns out to have a heart of gold." Jeff paused and then added, "It'll probably go straight to video."

"I'll be looking for it on the Disney Channel," Regan chuckled. As she gave him the details of their expected docking time and place, she visualized Jeff, the slight frown of concentration that creased his forehead, the thick dark brown hair, the hazel eyes, the mustache that he was always shaving off and growing back, the six-foot-three linebacker build. No question about it.

He was a hunk. "Okay then. I'll see you Saturday," Regan said, feeling a welcome boost. "I've got a lot to tell you."

"I'm looking forward to it," Jeff said.

"Me too."

Veronica bobbed up just as Regan replaced the receiver. "My dear, you should have called me. Who was that?"

"A friend I'll be seeing in New York."

"A man, I hope?"

"As a matter of fact, yes."

"I'm so glad. Regan, dear, you must be quite special to him if he phoned you all the way from New York."

"Believe me, Veronica, that doesn't necessarily mean a thing. I've had guys call me from halfway around the world who didn't call when they got home. Sometimes I think long distance is even better than being there.

"Where are their manners?" Veronica sighed. "I guess they threw away the mold when dear Gilbert entered this sphere. Well, let's be off to the psychic and see if she has any favorable predictions for our loving, yearning psyches."

Regan felt the chicken salad rise in her throat.

THE PSYCHIC SESSION with Madame Lily Spoker began promptly at two-thirty in the Theatre. Regan judged Madame Spoker to be about fifty years old, with large dark eyes, a generous Roman nose, a wide mouth, and brassy red hair that straggled out from an iridescent turban. She wore a v-necked rust-colored satin blouse which was not intended to conceal her swelling bosom, and a swirly multicolored skirt that swished in unison with the unmistakable sound of panty-hosed thighs vigorously chafing each other as she made her way to the lectern.

Regan had noticed Nora seated in the rear on the right and deliberately steered Veronica to the two vacant seats near Kenneth and Dale, who were settled in the first row on the left. Dale leaned over to them and raised his eyebrows. "We figured this was too good to pass up."

"Isn't this thrilling?" Veronica chirped. "Ssshhh. She's about to start."

Madame Spoker beamed at them. "I can tell this is going to be a most interesting and productive session. My vibrations are very strong. Many people come to psychic sessions to scoff. If some of you feel this way, I assure you when you leave you will not be scoffing.

"The heart has reasons of which reason knows nothing. I submit to you that the head also has reasons of which reason knows nothing. From eons ago, before time began, your fate was written in the stars. What you were, what you would be, was already decided." She threw out her arms and closed her eyes. "I know the questions in your minds. Why then, am I here?"

That's what I was wondering, Regan thought.

"I will tell you why—because to all of us is given, at defined points in our lives—a crossroads. If we do this, one scenario will follow. If we do something else, a far less favorable, perhaps even tragic, result will occur. I cannot believe that every one of you did not at some time have a premonition, a feeling, a warning that you ignored. That was your subconscious trying to point you toward the good path, to warn you of the perils of the other one."

Her voice dropped dramatically, became a near whisper.

"In most of us that secret voice is too still, too small, a weak faint cry against the tide." She threw out her fleshy arms in a sweeping gesture that embraced the room. "Today with my help you will hear the secret warnings of your subconscious." As she let her arms flop to her sides, which was not a very great distance, she looked around the room and waited for applause. Veronica did not disappoint her.

"Let's get started, Madame Spoker," Veronica cried as she clapped and squirmed in her seat.

"I want you all to write a question about your life on these pieces of paper I am passing out. I will then call you up one by one at which time you will hand me your folded paper and take a seat right here." Madame Spoker pointed to a lonely-looking chair on the bare stage. "This way I will be able to gather your own personal vibrations. I'm not going to look at the question—I will feel it."

Veronica started scribbling madly on her allotted scrap while Regan sat there wondering what the hell to ask this voodoo woman. Then it came to her. She leaned the paper on her purse and wrote, "Will we ever find Athena's murderer?" As she folded it up she realized this was a first in her years of detective work.

There was no way Madame Spoker could avoid calling Veronica up to the hot seat immediately. Veronica grabbed it as though it were the last one available in a game of musical chairs. "What do you feel for me?" she beseeched.

Madame Spoker crumpled Veronica's paper into a ball in

the palm of her hand, closed her eyes, and began to sway back and forth. "You are a very wise woman, Miss . . ."

"Exner. Lady Veronica Exner, widow of the late Sir Gilbert."

"Yes. I feel that peerage. You are a most giving person and much more savvy than people realize. You've had a long life . . ." She paused, shook, and opened her eyes.

"But what about my question?" Veronica asked.

Madame Spoker looked troubled. "It would be best if you come to my next session on Friday. I'm not getting a good enough reading on you right now. I need more time to concentrate on your magnetic field and I don't have it today. There are numerous people here and I want to give as many as possible a chance to come up. I promise you will be first on Friday."

Veronica looked disappointed but was a good sport and reclaimed her seat next to Regan.

Nice way to make sure people come back to your next hour of abracadabra, Regan thought. Abracadabra. It sounded like abracadaver.

Others came and went to the front of the room and Madame Spoker went through all the appropriate shaking and writhing motions. There was a group of girls from a cosmetics firm who were traveling together, all having won the trip for selling cases and cases of everything from lip gloss to eyebrow pencils to the ever-popular concealer stick. One of them, twentyish, with teased hair sprouting from every follicle on her scalp, and wearing a diamond engagement ring, was warned not to marry her fiancé.

"I see trouble there. There is something you don't know. He might take you to nice places but he's a *LIAR*! I'm sorry, but I feel so strongly about this, I must warn you."

As the distressed damsel returned to her seat, chewing furiously on a wad of gum, Regan heard her mumble, "Ah, what the hell does she know?" But she looked concerned. Poor guy, Regan thought. He probably put his life savings into that ring and will never get it back if his betrothed decides to heed the advice of Madame Spoker.

Next up, from the back of the room, came Immaculata Buttacavola. Nervously she took her place.

Madame Spoker beamed as she finally doled out some good news. "I think there's going to be an addition to your family very soon. In the next year, I'd say."

Immaculata clapped her hands and cried out, "My daughter-in-law Roz missed a period right before we left on our trip. Maybe they'll have an announcement when we get back." She got up from the chair. "Thank you, Madame, thank you," she gushed as she hurried to the back of the room. "Mario, I told you we should have bought that adorable baby T-shirt with the ship's insignia. Let's rush and see if they've got any left."

Veronica turned to Regan. "Isn't that lovely? I wonder what they'll name it."

Almost time for a new family portrait at Sears, Regan thought.

Veronica continued, "Regan, you haven't had your chance yet. Madame Spoker . . ."

"Of course. Miss, please join me."

Well at least she didn't call me ma'am, Regan thought as she got up and handed over her question.

Madame Spoker closed her eyes and started to hum, a low-grade staccato noise that sounded like an engine in trouble. Regan waited, wondering what she would "feel" for a question about a murderer.

"Something is close . . . I feel like you are closer to something or someone than you ever suspected. But there is danger. Stay out of harm's way." Madame Spoker rolled the paper around and around in the palm of her hand, the momentum increasing with the fluttering of her manicured fingers. She cried out, "Ouch. Damn it, I got a paper cut. They take so long to go away." Shaking her head, she resumed her humming.

A moment later her hand sprang open. Desperately she tried to close it over the folded question but her fingers seemed to be frozen. The scrap fell to the floor. The psychic jumped back from it as if it were a ticking bomb and started to shake. "I have never lost control of a question before. The power and vibrations coming from that little square of a dead tree are threatening to overwhelm me. Miss, you have asked a very serious question and I must warn you . . . you cannot be too careful. Dangerous people surround you. You will find what you are looking for, but the cost may be too great.''

Regan fervently wished her mother had opted for the two-thirty bridge lecture.

CAMERON HARDWICK SWAM furiously from one side of the deserted pool in the health spa to the other. It was small but he couldn't stand to be around a bunch of pesky kids jumping in and out of the larger pool on the Lido Deck, the younger ones being coaxed in and out by their goofy parents. It should be against the law to take kids on these ships. He winced again when he thought of the pictures taken at Chez Buttacavola.

That banquet manager from Atlantic City wasn't as big a dope as he looks, he thought to himself, surging into the butterfly stroke. God, it felt good to stretch and work his muscles. In the space of fifteen minutes this morning there had been two breaks from his desired anonymity. His gut felt as if it had twisted into a pretzel. He breathed in the scent of the chlorine and felt the water shimmering across his back. I have to cool it, he thought.

He reached the side of the pool, did a somersault underwater and reemerged as he now started the backstroke. Who would have thought that sitting in on some stupid finance lecture would result in that idiot Mario calling attention to him? Hardwick felt his blood start to boil again. Of all the lousy stinking luck. He could have throttled him. And now he had to see him every night at dinner. Willing himself not to let his volatile temper get the best of him, he realized that he was going to have to smooth things over with the dinner crowd. He couldn't wait until this job was over with. Wouldn't his old man be proud of him now? he thought angrily. I'm making money, Dad, but not the way you wanted me to. Selling drugs at his prep school twenty years ago had spoiled him for real work. Sure, this was high-risk, but the returns were better. And he liked living on the edge.

Today was Tuesday. The inactivity was driving him crazy. He started to think. Was it possible to make a move sooner than Friday? Should I wait for that one shot? On Friday night all the heavy luggage would be put out in the hallways, collected and stored for easy disembarkation early Saturday morning. Hardwick smirked. He had heard about a group of drunken waiters who, on one crossing, had wandered down the hallways the night before arriving, fished what they wanted out of a dozen suitcases, then merrily thrown them overboard. But they had been caught. He had no intention of letting that happen to him. Reilly's and Exner's suitcases would be picked up and the two of them wouldn't be missed until the ship was nearly empty, the luggage lay unclaimed on the pier, and he was long gone. As Hardwick pulled himself up out of the pool, he decided it was best to wait till Friday night. The less time they had to investigate the disappearance of the occupants of the Camelot Suite, the better.

Lady Exner undoubtedly would keep aside a bag of wrinkle cream and God knew what other useless potions to fight the aging process for use Saturday morning, which she would have to haul off the ship. He would just chuck it in the water after her, with whatever getup she was planning to greet her money-hungry nieces in. Let the sharks fight over her cigarettes.

Hardwick reached for his towel and started to dry his muscular arms. Reilly was the one who might cause him some trouble, he thought. She looked like a fighter, and being a detective, probably had a lot of street smarts. But those street smarts wouldn't help when he surprised her during her rapid-eye movement. He wasn't about to let any woman ruin his plans.

He stood before the mirror at the exit and combed back his shiny black hair. Pleased with his reflection, he bent down to slip on the lime-green water shoes he had bought for windsurfing. When he had worn these on the beach at the Jersey shore some idiot had called out, "Hey, Kermit, where's Miss Piggy?" Cameron had had to hold back from decking him. The only thing that had restrained him was the sight of a band of beer guzzlers stretched out on their towels, laughing, waiting for his reaction, only too eager to come to the aid of their ringleader. The Andrew Dice Clay Road Company.

Hardwick straightened up and wrapped his beach robe around his frame, tying it at the waist, grimacing at the feeling that the belt had a little more ground to cover than usual. The extra ounce or two was barely visible to the naked eye, but to him it was a perversion. He hated to have any pinchable flesh anywhere, especially around his stomach. Leave the love handles to the Marios of this world.

As he climbed the staircase back to his cabin, he felt content that his plans were complete. Turning onto his deck he almost bumped into a couple of giggling heavily made-up girls who batted their Tammy Faye Bakker eyes at him in admiration. Too bad I can't follow up with one of them to pass the time, he thought as he strode into the mini-corridor outside his door, and heard his phone ringing. Hurriedly he pulled his key out of his pocket and dashed inside.

The call was from Oxford.

I can't believe it's only Tuesday, Regan thought as she led Veronica into the Knights Lounge for bingo. She had seen the expression on her mother's face when the psychic became apoplectic. It was a Maalox moment for Nora.

Regan felt guilty about worrying her mother when she was supposed to be having a relaxing time on vacation. "I don't care how old you are, when we're under the same roof, I worry when you get in late," Nora would always say. "When you're in California, I don't know what you're up to and that's fine." Then she'd added, "But I do pray a lot."

I never should have accepted this job, Regan decided. I'm itching to work on Athena's case. I should have flown straight to New Jersey and dug out my journal. One night Athena had talked a lot about the last summer she'd spent with her aunt and uncle and cousins. She didn't talk only about the murder. I wrote down everything she told me.

"Regan dear, why don't we take this table here?" Veronica pointed to a low round table on the corner of the dance floor, surrounded by four seats. "Seeing as this is the Knights Lounge, maybe a few in shining armor will join us."

"Oh, I think the salt air would probably bother them too much, Veronica." Regan grinned, thinking back to the visit she and Kit had made to the armor factory in Graz, Austria. Kit had asked the tour guide if the factory had closed down because no knights had been sighted by the female population in hundreds of years.

As they sat down in the maroon-upholstered swivel seats,

Regan spotted Kenneth and Dale entering the lounge. She jumped up and called them over. "I never thought I'd see you two here."

"Oh, why not?" Dale answered cheerfully. "It's clouded over outside, so we figured we'd come in, have a drink, and hopefully win a few bucks."

"Oh, lovely," Veronica chirped. "Do sit down."

"Only if you pick out my playing cards, Lady Exner," Dale said. "I know you have that magic touch. The only thing Kenneth and I ever won was a six-month subscription to a Spanish-language newspaper, and needless to say, 'hola' and 'adiós, amigos' are the only words we understand."

Kenneth chimed in. "We ended up signing it over to our friend Carmen. She's from Madrid and lives next door. On Sundays she comes over for Dale's fabulous exotic coffee that no one else can make and she reads us the highlights."

"So it wasn't a total loss," Dale laughed as he beamed at Kenneth.

Scooping up everyone's money, Veronica joyfully got on line to purchase the cards, as the room began to fill with groups of twos, threes, and even singles who welcomed the chance to try their hand at one of the oldest forms of entertainment on land or at sea. Regan wondered how many church auditoriums, to this day, had someone calling out "N-33" or "O-77" every Friday night, eventually followed by someone screeching "Bingo!" It had been a favorite of Regan's grandmother.

The cruise director, Duncan Snow, whose ever-present smile reminded Regan of a jack-o'-lantern, picked up the mike and announced that they were about to "staht" and would the players please take their places.

Veronica sat back down, shuffled the cards, which were actually pieces of paper, and dealt them out with the finesse of a Vegas dealer. "There we go. Two each for the first go-around. And here are some pencils. No chips. Just circle the numbers that are called. Oh, here's the waitress. Let's order some drinks." She turned to Kenneth and Dale. "What would you like?"

The waitress, a twentyish brunette who looked as if she had

been partying late in the crew disco, took the order for four gin and tonics and disappeared.

". . . 6 and 6 clickety click. That's right, ladies and gentlemen. O-66 clickety click," Duncan Snow called, as oohs and ahs echoed through the room.

As he called out more numbers, Regan slowly realized that she was not the owner of a lucky card. Neither was anyone else in her group. Duncan announced "B-12."

A prepubescent voice at the next table yelled, "I got it, Mom. Bingo!" The assistant cruise director, Lloyd Harper, whom Regan guessed to be about her age, smiled at her as he passed her table on his way to check the boy's card. Regan smiled back at him, grateful that Veronica was still bent over, figuring out all the different ways she could have made bingo if she only had one more number.

More cards were purchased and games played with various ways of winning. The first person to form an *X* on his or her card would take the pot. The first to line the borders all around. The first to form an *L*. Finally Duncan announced that the next game would be the last and the jackpot was the biggest of the day. There was a scramble for more cards as people decided to buy two or three extra ones in the hopes of winning big money.

"This time the winner will be the first person to completely fill their card with circles. That's right. You have to get every number." Duncan looked delighted.

I wonder if there's any way they can fix this game, Regan thought. She had heard about the cruise director who was in cahoots with some bimbo on board. They used to pretend she had won and then they'd split the proceeds. She looked at the ten-year-old, who was still clutching his winnings. That kid wasn't going to split his hundred bucks with anyone.

Duncan began again to call the numbers, having a little expression or singsong for each one. "N-26, let's pick up sticks. Let's pick up sticks, N-26."

On the opposite side of the lounge Gavin was seated between two women of uncertain age. The knees of the one on the right were jammed against his. The one on the left had a disconcerting habit of poking her elbow into his arm whenever one of the numbers on her card came up. She repeated every number in a loud questioning voice, causing Gavin's blood pressure to rise as he yelled, "Yes, that's the number," to her, which in turn occasionally made him miss the next number called, which forced him to ask the people at the next table, which started the cycle all over again. He had also suffered the embarrassment of having her yell "Bingo!" when she wasn't even close.

I can't take much more of this, Gavin thought to himself. Let this be the last crossing I have to make, please. At least my card is filling in fast. Only two more numbers to go. As the next number was called and he energetically circled his next-to-last empty space on the card, he heard Lady Veronica's familiar trill, "Ooh, ooh, dear. Bingo! Isn't that lovely?" Them that has gets, he observed sourly as she literally danced to the mike, waving her card in her hand.

As Veronica hugged the cruise director, Lloyd Harper checked her numbers and announced that she had won $462. There was a round of oh-so-brief applause as people got up from their chairs, mumbling about coming back tomorrow to try and win the big money. "I told you I should have bought a couple of extra cards," Regan heard one old man admonish his wife. "She was in line right behind us and we would have gotten the winning one."

"Ah, shut up, Henry, you blame me for everything," the old woman wheezed. "Besides, you've got more money than you know what to do with. Lord knows you've never wasted any of it on me."

As Veronica stood at the front of the room chatting with Duncan while Lloyd counted out the money, Dale laughed. "Well, I knew she'd pick a winning card, I was just hoping it would be mine. By the way, Regan, she spoke to me about buying some antiques for Llewellyn Hall. Is she serious, or do you think that's just cocktail talk?"

"Well, she was talking about putting in some new plumbing

and rewiring ten years ago and she's just getting around to it now. You'd have to be Marco Polo to find the only loo in that house that works, and it groans for twenty minutes after you flush it. I think she means it when she says it, but I doubt she'll ever get around to any extensive redecorating."

"Oh, well," Kenneth lamented, "there goes our excuse for getting back to London this fall."

"It was a nice thought," Dale agreed. "But that's how I had her pegged. Exactly where in Oxford is Llewellyn Hall?"

"In the estate section," Regan replied.

"It's beautiful there. How much property does she have?"

"Something over five hundred acres."

"Are you joking?" Dale gasped.

"No, why?"

"About six years ago I worked with an interior designer who was doing a house in that area. The people had paid a fortune for only twenty acres. Veronica has that kind of money and she jumps up and down about winning a few hundred bucks?"

"Veronica and her nephew are two of the most unworldly people I've ever met," Regan answered. "Except for her trips, Veronica doesn't spend much money, and I don't think she realizes the value of that place. All her nephew cares about is sticking flowers in it."

"Who is going to inherit all that land?" Kenneth prodded.

Regan shrugged her shoulders. "I suppose the nephew."

"She told me she was going to visit some niece," Kenneth continued. "She asked me to fix her hair before she disembarks in New York."

"Actually she's a second cousin, who started to write to Veronica and sent her pictures of her family. Veronica has never met her but she sent pictures back of herself and her nephew and his fiancée and Llewellyn Hall."

"What does this second cousin do?" Dale asked.

"I gather she just lost her job, so she'll have time to take Veronica around." Regan frowned. "Veronica told me she had worked in a real estate office."

Kenneth raised his eyebrows for the second time in that hour.

"Well, somebody's head isn't in the clouds," Dale observed. "If I were the nephew, impractical or not, I'd be getting very nervous.

SYLVIE SASHAYED AROUND her cabin, spritzing perfume on her pulse points, singing "We're in the Money" with great gusto but not really knowing the words. ". . . oh that's right, honey, we're in the money toni-i-ight. You are so handsome . . . I am so pretty . . . doo doo doo . . . we're in the money . . . oh, that's right, honey . . . we'll get rid of old Violet . . . doo doo doo . . . as quick as a bunny . . ."

As Sylvie stepped into her cream-colored cocktail dress she realized she hadn't been so excited about a man for a long time. Too long. Milton was just so nice. And what a gentleman. Spending time with him today had had the double-edged sword of reminding her what she'd been missing since Harold died. Forget the other creep she'd married. He didn't count. But her life with Harold had been special.

This afternoon Milton had unknowingly brought on a resurgence of those feelings, of how right it can be when you're with someone and there's a chemistry. When the old bat Violet had finally gone to take a nap, losing round 2 to Sylvie and the ear patch, she and Milton had gone for a walk around the deck. He had taken off his sweater and put it around her shoulders when the wind started to pick up. She had felt like a high school cheerleader whose boyfriend had just given her his football jacket.

Don't get carried away, Sylvie thought to herself as she fastened the hook on her dress. But I do hope some of my perfume stayed on his sweater. When he wears it again he'll be reminded of me. Nothing like a smell to bring back memories. With my luck big sis will have borrowed it and he'll get it back smelling like Ben-Gay.

Sylvie glanced at her watch. Six forty-five. I'd better get going, she thought as she reflected on all the times when she'd felt so alone at these Captain's parties. How depressing. Well, tonight would be different. She had plans to meet up with Milton and Violet and would then introduce them to the people from her table, especially Lady Exner. If that failed, she'd enlist the help of Gavin to entertain the hardly shrinking Violet. That settled in her mind, she freshened her lipstick and started to sing "Tonight, tonight won't be just any night . . ."

Nora helped Luke with the studs on his tuxedo cuffs.

"I don't know how guys who live alone can get these things on," he commented.

"Well, I'm not going to let you have the chance to find out how they do it." Nora smiled up at him. "You look so handsome. Especially in black."

"As our daughter would say, it's good for business." Luke smiled back at her and leaned down for a kiss.

Nora frowned. "Luke, I'm so worried about her."

Luke realized he should never have brought Regan's name into the conversation. After the psychic session that afternoon, Nora had been a wreck. He had finally managed to talk some sense into her, and now it was about to start all over again. "Honey, it'll be just a few more days on the ship and then she'll be back at work, dealing with real criminals again. That's when we're allowed to worry. Not when she's minding a harmless old woman in the best suite on the ship." He hugged her. "Now go back to thinking about who she should have married."

Nora laughed reluctantly and gave him a playful punch. "All right, you. But I'll be relieved when we are all off this ship."

"Me too. I'm anxious to hear her opinion of my version of a green room."

* * *

Regan followed Veronica out of their suite. Not expecting to cruise home, Regan had not brought many dressy clothes on her trip. Clad in a deceptively simple black cocktail dress, she provided quite a contrast to Veronica's silver taffeta ball gown, the rejected outfit of the night before. All I need is a white apron and people will think I'm her traveling maid, Regan thought.

As the elevator door closed on the hoop of Veronica's dress, Regan pushed all the buttons in a frantic effort to save the dress from being ruined. She needn't have worried. When she finally managed to free Veronica's glad rags from the groaning, buzzing, jammed door, the hoop immediately sprang back into its original shape. It's crush-proof, Regan thought with amazement. That must have been ghosts of the fashion police trying to destroy it.

"Eeewwww," Veronica cried. "Thank you, Regan. I'm so glad it didn't rip."

Rip, Regan thought. That thing is made of U.S. Steel. "No problem at all. You look so pretty, Veronica."

"And so do you, my dear. But I would love to take you shopping and really dress you with some oomph. For example, you'd look lovely in a dress like this. Would you believe I bought it off the peg?"

Yes, Regan thought.

Gavin entered the Queen's Room with a nervous air. The band was playing softly in the background. The Captain and his senior management team, spit and polished in their dress whites, were ready to meet and greet the first-class passengers. The ship's photographer had his equipment set up, ready to snap passengers as they flanked the Captain. It was a great money-maker on these cruise lines. Even though the photos were outrageously priced, not many tourists could resist buying these mementos of their trip that went on sale as fast as the photography staff could get them out on display. Some people bought them to get their highly unflattering likenesses out of the display case where they were subject to the scrutiny of their fellow travelers.

I'd better do some good mixing tonight, Gavin thought anxiously. If I don't get that bracelet soon, I'll need a lot of spare time to spend only with Veronica. The apprehension sent a wave of anxiety sweeping through his body. He forced a smile and walked over to say hello to the Captain. Gavin reached out his hand. "Good evening, sir."

Thanks to the fact that Veronica was so anxious to get to the party, she and Regan were one of the first people on line to meet the Captain. Within a few minutes of their arrival, the line snaked out the door and past the Lancelot Bar. Dutifully the Captain put his arms around both of them as Veronica twittered "cheese." Though the Captain did his best to be charming, Regan was relieved after the usual pleasantries were exchanged. As Veronica attempted to linger with him, Regan accepted a glass of champagne from a passing waiter and looked around. The early birds had already staked out seats on the couches and chairs that formed a horseshoe around the dance floor.

"Oh, Regan, over here!" Regan turned to her left and saw Sylvie waving to them. She was seated on one of the couches next to an older woman.

"Veronica, let's go over and say hello to Sylvie."

"Lovely, dear. Carry on."

As they made their way over, the band started to play a version of "Chattanooga Choo-Choo" complete with swishy sounds made by the drummer's instrument that looked like a miniature broom. Even though most people her age hated this kind of music usually played at weddings, Regan did get a kick out of it. She noticed one couple out on the dance floor as they started their own little two-step, joining hands and twirling, knowing each other's moves without even looking, gracefully dancing together as they probably had been doing for the past forty years. By the time I celebrate my fortieth anniversary with someone, Regan thought, the only way we'd be able to move around the dance floor together would be if someone wheeled us back and forth out there. A dancer and a waiter both tripped on Veronica's hoop before they reached Sylvie.

"Lady Exner." The woman seated next to Sylvie looked up worshipfully.

"Yes, Sir Gilbert Exner's widow." Veronica seemed delighted that someone finally recognized her status before she had to inform them.

Introductions were made and Veronica sat down on the chair nearest Violet. Sylvie is glowing, Regan thought as she sat down in the chair opposite Veronica and next to Milton.

As the room filled, white-gloved waiters passed champagne, the band played on, and the noise level increased to that of a full-blown cocktail party. Chatter and laughter filled the air as people appraised each other's outfits and finally got the chance, in the convivial atmosphere, to say hello to fellow passengers they had not yet met.

Cameron Hardwick leaned against a column sipping his champagne and sneaking an occasional glance over at Veronica and Regan. The future flotsam and jetsam, he thought to himself. Hopefully she doesn't wear that gown to bed Friday night. It would serve as a parachute on the way down the side of the ship. She'd stay afloat for days. He turned away when he saw the old biddy from this afternoon pointing him out to Veronica. Jesus, he thought angrily. I don't need those two comparing notes.

". . . I just know that that young man waited on us in Greece, over ten years ago," Violet confided to Veronica. "It was after my dear Bruce died. He insisted this afternoon when I mentioned it to him that he'd never been to Greece, but I know for sure he's mistaken. It was August 1981. We had a window table and I ordered stuffed shrimp, but they were out of it. When I couldn't make up my mind what to order, he got very impatient with me. And to think we were paying top dollar to stay in that hotel," Violet said haughtily.

"We were discussing Greece at dinner last night and he told us he'd never been there," Veronica replied.

"I'm telling you I know it was he," Violet harrumphed. "I never forget a face."

Veronica smiled. "He's really quite nice. He took me for a stroll on the deck last night and offered his arm. So protective! Maybe you'd like to query him again on Thursday evening. I've decided to have a cocktail party in our suite before dinner. I'm inviting everyone from my table and I would be enchanted if you and your brother would join us. I'd love to show you pictures of Sir Gilbert and Llewellyn Hall."

Violet looked as if the boil on her behind had finally burst. "We'd be happy to be your guests."

MEANWHILE, BACK AT the ranch, Regan thought as she took her seat at the dinner table. Here we all are to share our experiences of the first full day at sea. It didn't take too long for the sharing to start.

"Have any of you ever been wrapped in seaweed?" Immaculata began. "I highly recommend it. It's a most tingly and refreshing experience."

Veronica interjected, "It sounds fascinating. What does it involve?"

It involves stripping the seven seas of every last trace of plant life to cover the frames of people who are too lazy to exercise, Gavin thought.

"Well," Immaculata continued excitedly, "you have to make an appointment at the beauty parlor downstairs. But you better do it soon because they are filling up their appointment book fast."

"Regan, we must remember to call first thing in the morning," Veronica rejoiced as she waved the resurrected cigarette holder.

"Even though it smells a little fishy," Immaculata said as she wrinkled her nose, "it's so worth it. They cover your body from head to toe in a creamy green masque, wrap you in plastic and thermal blankets, and leave you to rest for a half hour while the seaweed flushes the toxins from your pores. After you shower it off, you get a massage while you listen to the music of your choice. I tell you, I feel like a new woman."

"I told her that was fine, just as long as she stays, deep down, the same Immaculata Marie I married," Mario announced as he buttered his roll. "I don't want you running off with one of the ship's officers now."

Fat chance, Hardwick thought.

Immaculata patted his back and laughed, "Oh, Mario," and proceeded to tell about her facial. "The thing that kills me is that they think by insulting your skin they'll get you to buy all their products. The girl told me I have problems with my capillaries and then did a pitch for a cream that costs seventy-five dollars. Can you believe that?"

Mario grunted. "Well, you bought it, didn't you, honey?"

"How could I resist? They guaranteed my skin would be baby-soft and smooth by the time I used up the tube."

It's not as if you can even return it if it doesn't work, Regan thought. The ship will be floating around the south seas by the time you figure out your capillary problems are irreversible.

"Did you know," Immaculata continued unabated, "that it's very important to brush your skin every morning with a natural-bristle brush? Our skin should shed over two pounds of flakes a day."

"So they sold her one of those brushes that they just happened to have on sale for another thirty-five bucks," Mario muttered as he examined a sesame-seed breadstick.

"Oh, Mario," Immaculata said as she patted his cheek. "Honestly, sloughing our skin is so important. Especially around the rough spots like your elbows, your heels, your knees. That's why you must exfoliate when you get up in the morning and when you go to bed at night . . ."

Gavin wondered if the salon played "Old MacDonald Had a Farm" when they brushed their clients.

". . . the girl told me that by the time the average person throws out their mattress, it weighs an extra twenty-five pounds. And that's from all the dead skin that's accumulated. It's like sleeping with a dead body," Immaculata said emphatically.

It'd be more exciting than sleeping with my ex-wife, Gavin thought.

Cameron Hardwick could barely contain himself. He pressed his lips closed.

"Cameron, dear," Lady Exner piped up, "I've been spreading the word. Thursday night Regan and I will be hosting a cocktail party before dinner in our suite. I hope you will make it. We have a thrilling view that's to die for . . ."

I know you do, Hardwick thought darkly. He smiled at her. "Thank you. I'll be there." How perfect. The suite across the hall is probably a mirror image, but now I'll know for sure what to expect Friday night.

"Lovely," Veronica cried. "That means that everyone here will be in attendance, along with a few other friends we've made today and perhaps a few more we have not yet met. After dinner I'm going straight upstairs to plan which hors d'oeuvres we will serve."

"That's my specialty," Gavin quivered, like a pot of water the second before it finally boils. "I planned a lot of the celebrity parties my radio station sponsored. As a matter of fact"—he turned and winked at Regan—"one famous author who shall remain nameless adored the scallops and bacon I always ordered for our annual Christmas bash . . ."

I think Nora went to that party once, Regan thought.

"And of course on board ship I have helped many of our guests plan private soirees. Lady Exner, please allow me to assist you this evening. I'm sure Regan might like the chance to join some of the younger folks down at the disco . . ."

What younger folks? Regan thought.

Gavin realized his armpits were drenched and he felt light-headed as Veronica agreed heartily. "You are too, too kind," she cried. "How lucky we are to have been placed at your table. Aren't we lucky, Regan?"

"Very lucky."

"I'm sure Regan would welcome the opportunity to expand

her horizons by socializing in the disco this evening. Wouldn't you, Regan?"

"I am always looking to expand my horizons."

"Good. It's settled then. Mr. Gray will make party plans with me and you will go forward and mingle." Veronica made a sweeping motion with her hands. "Maybe you'll dance with that young man who smiled at you during bingo."

"PIGS IN A blanket have always been a favorite hors d'oeuvre of mine," Veronica pronounced as she plopped down next to Gavin on the pastel couch, "although I'm afraid some people find them common. Sir Gilbert loved them to excess. I shall never forget the time he popped one in his mouth and his eyes took on a glazed look. I panicked and started pounding on his frail back. This was before the Heimlich Maneuver was invented."

Gavin waited expectantly for the final word on Sir Gilbert's fate.

Veronica sighed. "Turns out he was fine. Just taking a little snooze with his eyes open. It happens more and more as one gets older. It was very near the end for him and the poor dear's health was failing rapidly. I was just glad that he had the chance to enjoy one of his favorite treats just days before he departed this planet for points unknown." Veronica paused, opened the special menu for private parties and smiled to herself. "Happily he enjoyed his favorite treat in the world just moments before he died."

Veronica turned to him with a glow in her eyes. "You're a very attractive man." She raised her eyebrows expectantly.

I was afraid it might come to this, Gavin thought fretfully. I'll have to head her off at the pass. Damn it, I'll have earned every last penny I get for that bracelet. He spotted a bottle of mineral water on the bar.

"Speaking of health," he stammered as he fumbled out of his seat and over to the bar. "I'll bet you haven't had your six to eight glasses of water today. Allow me to pour you one."

"In a setting such as this I prefer champagne," Veronica cooed.

Gavin lunged for glasses, twisted open the dark green bottle of Pellegrino and hurriedly poured its sparkling contents, causing it to bubble up and overflow. Grabbing a cocktail napkin, he mopped it up. "But this has bubbles too and you can drink so much more of it." He laughed with nervous relief as she beamed and accepted it from him. She had had a couple of whiskey sours, wine, and a cappuccino at dinner, he calculated rapidly. A couple of these should send her scurrying to the loo, and with any luck that dress will take minutes to negotiate around the toilet seat.

Settling back on the couch, Veronica patted the cushion next to her and motioned to Gavin. "Besides the pigs in a blanket, it's always good to have a wheel of Brie at a party, don't you think?"

Relieved to move through the ship on her own, Regan wandered through the casino, hoping to spot her parents. They were already gone from the dining room when her table got up, and she had phoned them, but as expected they were not in their room. As she walked by the slot machines, a bell rang, followed by the tinny sound of quarters dropping into the tray of the machine that had just lined up the winning combination of three cherries in a row. An expressionless man with a chewed-up cigar hanging out of the side of his mouth scooped up the quarters and dropped them back in his paper cup. No matter how much you win at those one-armed bandits, Regan thought, most people keep playing until they've used up all their change. Regan had heard it was best to play the machines near the entrances. The victorious sound of the ringing bells attracts people wandering by, and no doubt the cruise line hopes they'll respond like Pavlov's dogs.

The blackjack tables were full and Regan noticed that Cameron Hardwick was already settled in at one and a waitress was serving him a drink. I don't want to get involved with him, Regan thought. Fixing her eyes straight in front of her she kept walking, exiting the casino and passing through the corridor with the photo displays, which tomorrow would be filled with the smiling faces of those who attended the Captain's party tonight. She remembered that Veronica said they must order extra pictures as she was sure her cousins would want a copy as well as Philip and Val. "Val recently dug out some of the old family pictures in the attic," Veronica had said, "and is having them framed. Except, of course, the pictures of Sir Gilbert's first wife. She looked like a pleasant enough lady, but I don't really need to be reminded that there was ever anyone else in Sir Gilbert's life. Too bad, because there is a striking one of Sir Gilbert as a young man, but she is in it and although I understand she was very good to him right up until the time she died, who needs to look at her?"

Regan reached the door of the Knights Lounge and looked in. It amazed her the way it took on a whole other aura in the evening. The lights were low, candles flickered on the tables, and the people who had played bingo in this room a few hours ago in their shorts were now all dressed up.

No wonder romance flourished at night, Regan thought. People look better by candlelight. It certainly was the subject of many songs. "Will You Still Love Me Tomorrow?" Gee, probably not.

A magician had just finished his routine and thankfully did a disappearing act himself. The band struck up and couples took to the floor as the female singer crooned, "Ohhhhh, did you tell her you lovvvveeee her? . . . andddd that you miss her so badlyyyyyyy . . ." Time to go down to the disco, Regan thought, and locate all the "younger folks." I may as well check out what the bar scene is like in the middle of the Atlantic.

Grabbing the railing of the back staircase as the ship took a sudden dip to one side, Regan felt oddly relaxed. She enjoyed having a little time to herself to think. Dinner had been long and she didn't feel like any more conversation for conversation's sake.

Regan took a place at one of the tables set back from the dance floor. Strobe lights revolved around and around, making colored circles and dots on the ceiling, floor and walls. As if there isn't enough movement on this ship to make you seasick, she thought. The music was blasting as it only could at a disco. "So many men, so little time . . ." Not the problem here, Regan thought, surveying the room. So few men, so much time. On land she would have hated going into a place like this alone, but there was something about life on board ship that changed all the rules. "We're all on this journey together, making new friends who we'll send Christmas cards to for the rest of our lives," the Captain had said in one of his fireside chats over the public address system. Clearly, the Captain loved the sound of his own voice. They had already been subject to several of his monologues and it was only the second day out. Any excuse and he would grab his microphone. He got on to tell them exactly where they were, how many nautical miles they had traveled, how far away was the closest land, et cetera. When Regan looked out the window, it always looked the same, no matter what information the Captain had shared. What was that saying? . . . "Water, water everywhere, and not a drop—"

"A drink, ma'am?"

Regan looked up. Ma'am. I'll kill him. She ordered a vodka and tonic from the young waiter who sported a crew cut and a handlebar mustache. Opening her purse, she reached for her notebook. Jotting down thoughts that were fresh in her mind had become second nature to her. Now she wrote "Livingston/sympathy note." Tomorrow she'd ask Livingston for the address of Athena's parents. She wanted to write to them.

"Hello."

Regan looked up and smiled at Lloyd, the bingo aide-de-camp. He was standing over her, looking tall and boyishly handsome in his whites. Nothing like a man in uniform, Regan thought.

"Mind if I join you?"

"Not at all," Regan replied as she slipped her notebook back into her purse.

My God, she must be a camel, Gavin thought as he poured yet another glass of water for Veronica, who showed no telltale signs of bladder strain. Either that or she's invested in a box of Depends. A half hour ago he had been practically doubled over in pain and used the facilities himself, but she seemed oblivious to the call of nature.

Veronica had finished circling her selections from the party menu. "I do hope these hors d'oeuvres are tasty enough. Since I'm not at home with my own secret ingredients, I won't be able to doctor them up. A true chef knows how to fuss with a dish and make it more interesting. And now, Mr. Gray, we must figure out how many people I've invited so we can order accordingly. Do you think we should invite some of the ship's officers, maybe even the Captain?"

I don't care, Gavin thought wildly, his eyes riveted on the closet door. Pee, damn it. PEE!

Veronica rushed on, "I'd love to finally be at a party where there are more men than women. We've already invited everyone at the table, which should be pleasant. I just hope that Cameron Hardwick is in a festive mood. I must remember to tell Regan that Violet Cohn insists she met him in Greece several years ago. Mr. Gray, what are you staring at?"

Lloyd was a good dancer. Regan realized she was enjoying herself. But when the set ended and he proposed a walk on the deck, she glanced at her watch and said, "I'd better get upstairs. I don't like to be away from Lady Exner for too long."

Harper looked disappointed but said, "I guess you're right. I saw her almost fall over the side yesterday. And it's been known to happen."

* * *

"I think we have everything in order, Mr. Gray. This is going to be such a good show." Veronica turned as she heard Regan's key in the door. "Oh, lovely, Regan's back. I wonder who she's talking to out there."

Another chance shot to hell, Gavin thought with an ever-escalating level of frustration felt inside his pounding head. Glass after glass of the bubbling water had given him a headache.

Regan entered, smiling.

"Regan, did you have a nice time?" Veronica asked gleefully.

"Veronica, you got your wish. The guy from bingo asked me to dance."

"Ooh, I can't wait to hear about it," Veronica said eagerly, "but first, if you'll excuse me."

Gavin sat there in disbelief as he watched her slam the bathroom door shut.

"Thank you," Regan said to him as she took a seat. "You're so nice to help out with the party planning."

Gavin's smile was a grimace of pain. "The pleasure was all mine." He stood up. "I'll let you two have a chance to chat before bed. Tomorrow morning please bring her to the Sit-and-Be-Fit class again. I'll be there . . . probably every day this week. Now I must really be going."

He let himself out. Regan took off her clothes and put on a robe. Veronica re-emerged and queried, "Where is Mr. Gray?"

"I think he was tired. He said he'll see you in the morning."

"Poor fellow must be. He's so thoughtful, but tonight I caught him just staring into space. He takes his responsibilities on this ship so seriously that he's busy from early in the morning until late at night." Veronica turned for Regan to unzip her dress. "I had to use the facilities so desperately, but he's so generous with his time I didn't want to leave him for a moment. It was embarrassing enough having to go this morning. Naturally I turned on the tap."

Veronica retreated into the dressing area as Regan pulled out the couch.

"You can't go to sleep, Regan, until you tell me all about your adventures tonight. Perhaps you should invite this young man to our party—it's going to be smashing. I'm sure everyone would love to have the chance to meet him . . ."

Regan pulled the covers over her head and thought, three and a half days to go.

Wednesday, June 24, 1992

BRIGHT SUNLIGHT STREAMED through their portholes as Luke and Nora sat in companionable silence, sipping their morning coffee and sharing the miniature shipboard newspaper that was slipped under their door each day.

"Darling, what should we plan to do today?" Nora asked as she picked up a copy of the Daily Program.

A knock at the door precluded a response.

"Could it be? . . ." Nora asked as Luke opened the door.

"I want my CAWFEE," Regan yelled, imitating Nora's roommate from a brief hospital stay earlier in the year.

"Well, come in and shut the door before the men in their white jackets take you away," Nora laughed.

"One almost did last night."

"What, dear?"

"Never mind," Regan mumbled as she slumped in the chair opposite Nora and poured herself a cup from their breakfast cart. "There's nothing like the third cup of the day."

"It's okay, I was finished anyway," Luke said wryly as he sat down on the love seat.

"Oh, sorry, Dad. If you don't mind, I'm going to put through another phone call, so sit here."

Nora looked curious. "Who are you calling now?"

"The Inspector in Oxford again. I want to see if he had any luck with getting the newspapers from Greece." Regan frowned. "Isn't it too much of a coincidence that two people from the same family were murdered within months of each other? I don't know. There's got to be a connection."

"Regan, what are you saying?" Nora asked quietly.

"I guess I'm hoping that something in those Greek papers will jump out at me."

Nora hesitated. "I've always taught you to trust your instincts, but after the way that psychic reacted to you yesterday—Regan, she was afraid for you."

"Mom, that woman is a quack. You know what she's doing today?" Regan did not wait for an answer. "Running a scarf-tying session. Give me a break. The next thing you know she'll be selling crystal balls with the *Queen Guinevere* logo. I bet she just needed a free ride across the Pond." Regan scooped up blueberry-muffin crumbs from Luke's plate and dropped them into her mouth.

Nora handed her a napkin as Regan got up and walked over to the phone. "Besides," she added quietly, "even though we weren't close, I wish I had made more of an effort with Athena . . ."

Oxford

CARRYING A PIPING-HOT cup of tea, Nigel Livingston walked down the drab hallway of the police station in Oxford, heading for the last door on the left, his office. My home away from home, he mused, with pictures of his wife and daughter adorning his massive desk. He quickened his pace when he heard his phone ringing, causing the steaming brew to spill over onto his stubby fingers. "Oh, buggers," he muttered angrily as the tea dripped down the side of the cup and splashed onto the gray tile floor.

The call was from Regan Reilly. "Just a second, Miss Reilly." With the receiver in one hand, Livingston circled his desk and sat down on his swivel chair. The file on the Popolous case was open on his desk. The first faxes from Greece had just arrived. He had spread them all out, anxious to read the new material as well as go over his notes, when he had gone for the cup of tea.

On the other end, Regan held out her cup as Luke freshened it with the last few drops of coffee in the pot. "Thanks, Lukey."

"Beg your pardon?" Nigel asked.

"Oh, sorry," Regan replied. "I'm calling from my parents' room. They're heading home from a trip to Europe and coincidentally were booked on this same crossing."

"Didn't I hear your mother is a mystery writer?"

"Yes. And by the way, I haven't told Lady Exner she's on board. She's rather anxious for my mother to write the story of her life. She can be quite determined."

"I understand," Livingston replied as he remembered the discussion he'd had yesterday with Philip Whitcomb and his fiancée. "Has Lady Exner expressed any concern for Miss Atwater's condition?"

"Not really. Although she did say that it was probably better Penelope wasn't along. With all the food they serve here, Penelope would have been eating day and night and ended up with a perpetual case of heartburn. Veronica said there's nothing more frustrating than traveling with someone who's always sick and complaining." Regan twirled the cord in her fingers, suddenly uneasy. "Why do you ask?"

"To get right to the point, do you think Veronica might have tried to eliminate Miss Atwater?" Livingston asked.

"Absolutely not."

"Then let's put it a different way," Livingston continued. "From all accounts, Miss Atwater had become something of a nuisance to Lady Exner. Do you think that she might have wanted to make it impossible for Miss Atwater to travel?"

Regan thought to herself, I suppose it's possible, but replied, "I don't believe that."

"I notice some hesitation in your voice, Miss Reilly."

"It's not meant to be there. I didn't even tell her about the arsenic found in Penelope's system because I didn't want to worry her. As far as Veronica knows, Penelope is suffering from a case of food poisoning, nothing more."

"I was over at Llewellyn Hall yesterday and Philip Whitcomb and his fiancée mentioned that Lady Exner had joked about sprinkling a bit of the arsenic on those hors d'oeuvres."

"Philip mentioned that?" Regan sounded incredulous.

"Well, Miss Twyler brought it up first. Which brings me to another matter. I saw your classmate Claire James yesterday, and again she talked about Athena taking a fancy to Philip. She says Athena had bicycled past Llewellyn Hall to see him. Do you think Philip could have been even a little keen on Athena?"

Regan furrowed her brows. "I really don't think so, but I just can't be sure. Athena and I never really did anything together. Claire has a talent for ferreting out that kind of information. She was always in the middle of whatever gossip was going on in the dorm, who was dating whom, whose boyfriend from the States was coming to visit . . ."

"That's rather the impression I get." Livingston glanced down at his notes. "One final thing. In Miss Popolous's jacket pocket we found a matchbook from the Bull and Bear with initials and a few numbers on it. We're trying to track that down and see if we come up with anything useful. Do the initials 'B.A.' mean anything to you?"

B.A., Regan thought. B.A. "I don't think so."

"How about the numbers three-one-five?"

"No . . ."

"Well, in the meantime I've just received the first set of faxes from Greece. Athena's small home town newspaper in Skoulis is published every Wednesday, which is today, so we should have the translated version of that by tomorrow. Hopefully you'll have the first lot sometime this morning."

"Good. If anything strikes me about B.A. or three-one-five while I'm reading the papers, I'll give you a call." Then she remembered to ask for the address of Athena's parents. She hung up, sure she would have to field questions from her parents about the suspicion cast on Veronica.

"I should get some faxes today," she told them quickly. "Right now they're just trying to follow whatever leads they can. I'd better go get Veronica and bring her to the poetry seminar. What are you two up to?"

Nora's expression changed. "I was going to go to that as well, but I think I'll pass. Let's see what else they have listed. Oh dear, they're having a contest at that time for all the grandparents on board . . . they're giving out prizes for whoever has the oldest grandchild, whoever has the youngest . . . maybe we'll be eligible for that in a couple of years . . ."

"Good-bye, folks," Regan muttered as she shut the door behind her, wishing for the umpteenth time she were one of ten children at least one of whom had made her an aunt by now.

At Sea

"REGAN! YOO-HOO! THERE you are!" Veronica cried as she and her fellow Sit-and-Be-Fitters extricated their hindquarters from their seats.

Regan decided that just as the gymnast has the uneven bars, a hockey player his stick, and the bodybuilder his barbells, these athletes had all the equipment they needed for their favored sport—a folding chair. "Yes, here I am," she agreed. "How was class?"

"Splendid. Did you enjoy it, Mr. Gray?"

"Oh yes," Gavin smiled, having awakened this morning with all the hope a new day can bring, feeling a fresh surge of energy to accomplish his mission, no matter what. "But, Regan, you didn't have to come down here. I told you we'd meet you back at the room . . ."

"Oh, that's all right. Veronica said she wanted to go to the poetry seminar. I thought we might take a look at the pictures from last night and then head straight there." Regan turned to Veronica. "Unless of course you need to go back to the suite."

"Certainly not. Mr. Gray, take some time for yourself. Ohhh, I can't wait to see the pictures. Come along, Regan. Thank you, Mr. Gray, we'll see you later."

As they walked off, Regan couldn't help but notice how Gabby Gavin's smile had crumpled. Could he be that disappointed about not walking Veronica back? Why?

A half hour later, with six pictures tucked under her arm, including several candid shots from the Captain's party which contained no one she knew but would be good to "show off the lovely atmosphere," Veronica paraded into the library where the poetry seminar was about to begin.

"Regan, I don't know why you didn't have me order an extra photo of you for your parents. I'm sure they would love one."

"Oh, Veronica, they have plenty of pictures of me. Being their first and only child, they recorded every event in my life, no matter how insignificant."

"Oh, how I would have loved to have had a child," Veronica sighed. A look of genuine sadness was evident on her face.

Glancing at her, Regan felt a stab of pain in sympathy. Veronica always kept up such a cheerful front that Regan never really entertained the thought that she had probably known plenty of disappointment in her life.

"However," Veronica continued, "since Sir Gilbert's first marriage of over fifty years did not produce an heir, I've sometimes reflected on the possibility that he was firing blanks."

Good old Veronica, Regan thought. Back to your old self in no time.

At the librarian's desk, the poet, a little man who looked like the Pillsbury Doughboy with black glasses, white button-down shirt, Bermuda shorts, black ankle socks and wing-tip shoes, began to address the group.

"From the time I was very young," Byron Frost proclaimed in a nasal voice, "I always liked to write poetry. My fifth-grade teacher got us started by having us write haikus. Does everyone know what a haiku is?"

"It's Japanese," Veronica responded. "It's a three-line poem with five syllables in the first and third lines and seven in the second. And it doesn't rhyme!"

"Yes, that's right. And it takes discipline. Before the end of class we're each going to write one. But I want to start off by saying that you should write about what you know or what you feel strongly about. For example, I wrote an ode to my lovely wife Georgette, which I will recite for you right now." He took off his glasses, folded his hands in a reverential manner, and lovingly looked over at a woman who Regan guessed had to be Mrs. Frost. "Georgette, my rare love . . ."

The lovely Mrs. Frost sat enthralled listening to her husband. As Regan watched her she was reminded of what Claire had said about Athena being mesmerized by Philip's poetry readings. The scene of Philip saying to her years ago, "It's one of the hazards of being an heiress . . . she'll be back . . ." kept replaying itself in Regan's mind. And now the Inspector was asking again if she thought there had been anything between Philip and Athena. Her body was found in the woods next to the Exner property. Regan realized her mind was darting between Oxford and Greece. Maybe the faxes will be here when we get back to the room, she thought. I need something tangible.

"Does anyone here have any poems that they would like to recite?" the emotionally spent Byron Frost asked of the flock.

Even before Veronica sprang to her feet, Regan braced herself, knowing Sir Gilbert was about to be resurrected.

"My dear departed husband Sir Gilbert Exner was a poet. Anytime and anyplace he would make up poems. When we were in bed he would hold me in his arms and recite his favorite creations. Moments before he died, he gathered me close and whispered his last original verse:

> *"I would like to say, say, say*
> *In a special way, way, way . . ."*

Nay nay nay, Regan thought.

THE STEWARD HAD left a manila envelope propped up on the dresser in the suite.

"For you, Regan," Veronica pronounced, glancing at it. "How sweet. An admirer, I hope. It will just take me a minute to change." She disappeared into the bathroom.

Regan ripped open the envelope. Photocopies of news stories from several Greek newspapers were enclosed with English translations. Thank God, she thought as she dropped them into her tote bag. They had elected to have a hamburger by the grill instead of a formal lunch.

When Veronica emerged from the bathroom she was sporting a striped red-and-white T-shirt, matching shorts and red sandals. She gathered up her sunscreen, her Jackie-O sunglasses and the latest book by Nora Regan Reilly.

At the pool they managed to find two deck chairs that were not already occupied or "saved" by the presence of a towel. Getting settled in her chair, Regan glanced at the ship's wake. We're in the middle of the ocean, she thought. She tried to imagine what it would be like to be lost at sea.

"This picture of your mother is lovely," Veronica pronounced as she studied the back cover of Nora's latest effort. "You do resemble her. I feel I'd know her anywhere."

That's what I'm afraid of, Regan thought.

Veronica opened the book. "I'm so happy to be reading this book while I'm with you, Regan. Now if I have any questions I can go practically to the source and find out all the inside information on the rascals and murderers I'll meet in here," Veronica said gaily as she flipped the pages from the back to the front with her thumb. "And now you must get to work."

Regan smiled absently and reached for the faxes in her bag. She unfolded them in her lap and began to read. The first headline, "Tragedy Strikes Prominent Family Twice," was followed by, "The decomposed body of Athena Popolous was discovered over the weekend in a wooded area in Oxford, England . . ." The columnist had an in-depth gossipy story worthy of the supermarket tabloids. "Nearly eleven years ago, Miss Popolous's aunt, Helen Carvelous, was murdered when she unexpectedly returned home as a burglary was taking place. Her death was also caused by strangulation. Priceless antique jewelry was stolen. Miss Popolous had been very close to her aunt and was most distraught." Regan stopped reading for a moment. We were just talking about stolen jewelry the other night at dinner, she thought, and somebody said something about antique jewelry. Gabby? No. Who? It would come back to her.

Reading on, Regan learned that Athena, the youngest by ten years in her immediate family, had often been left with servants by her parents. She had adored her aunt, spent every possible moment with her and her children, and, as the article put it, "seemed to blossom when she was in that joyous, loving atmosphere."

I wish I had understood, Regan thought sadly. Why didn't she ever tell me she had been that close to her aunt? Athena's parents had been abroad that summer and she was living with her aunt when the tragedy occurred. Regan studied the picture of Athena's family. Her sisters and brother were all in their forties now and very attractive. Athena had obviously taken after her heavyset father, inheriting his broader features. Her brother Spiros was quoted as saying, "After my aunt died, we thought a change of scenery would be best for Athena. We sent her to school in England in the hopes that it would help her recover. Obviously we never thought it would end in another tragedy."

Helen's now eighteen-year-old daughter was quoted, "I always thought of Athena as a big sister. She spent a lot of time with us. The day my mother died our governess had joked to her that she didn't really feel needed because Athena was always helping out. But my mother didn't care because she thought it was more important we were learning English from the governess."

Carefully Regan read the remaining articles. They were all similar to the first one. This wasn't much help. Maybe the local paper, which Livingston had said should arrive tomorrow, might be more useful. Local papers tended to be chatty.

"Anything interesting?" Veronica asked. "I'm so sorry for that poor dear girl."

"Nothing helpful. But I'll be getting more faxes from Greece tomorrow." Regan sighed as she put them away.

"All this talk about Greece. I forgot to tell you that Violet Cohn insisted to me that she had met Cameron Hardwick in Greece. Even though he denies it, she says he was a waiter there."

"When was that, Veronica?"

"Eleven years ago."

"MARIO AND I are having such a wonderful time," Immaculata pronounced as appetizers were being served. "Tonight at the midnight buffet they are going to unveil a big replica of the Statue of Liberty carved out of butter. We don't want to miss it. To think that Mario's parents and my grandparents all immigrated to America and Miss Liberty was there to welcome them. It gives me tingles. Mario, let's not forget to bring the camera."

"Uh-huh," Mario grunted as he dug into his Alaskan crabmeat on toast.

Most people here look pretty content, Regan thought. Sylvie is smiling. Regan had seen her heading into the movie theater after lunch with Violet Cohn and her brother. Dale's and Kenneth's tans had grown deeper, thanks to an afternoon spent lounging by the pool in the sunny weather that was not typical of a North Atlantic crossing. Veronica had enjoyed the scarf-tying session and another round of bingo even though she didn't win today. She had busied herself inviting all the staff members there to her party, including Lloyd, who had been busy counting the money. Gabby Gavin seemed a little preoccupied and edgy. They hadn't seen much of him since that morning, but had waved to him across the room at bingo. And then, of course, there was Cameron Hardwick.

Sipping her Chardonnay, Regan asked, "What did you do today, Cameron?"

He shrugged. "I went down to the gym to lift weights and

take a swim. I hate it when I don't get enough exercise." He broke a roll in half with his large, strong-looking hands.

You didn't have to come on a cruise to lift weights, Regan thought. She watched Veronica put out her cigarette in the ashtray she shared with Mario. Suddenly she realized that she had never seen Hardwick smoke. Why would someone who professed to be health-conscious sit at a smoking table? For my taste, there's too much that doesn't make sense about that guy, Regan thought. As she glanced at the Rolex watch on his wrist she wondered if those hands had ever cleared plates from restaurant tables in Greece. It was hard to imagine him taking orders from anyone.

"Now, don't forget, everyone, tomorrow night at five o'clock we're having our cocktail party," Veronica said eagerly. "We'll have a couple of hours to socialize before dinner. I'm going to have everyone there write down their address and I'll have the list Xeroxed on Friday so that we can all keep in touch."

Regan noticed that only Mario and Immaculata seemed to think it was a wonderful idea. She had a vision of a succession of Christmas cards featuring Mario the Third and Concepcione standing before a fireplace, Christmas stockings dangling over their heads.

Thursday, June 25, 1992

"REGAN, IT'S TIME to get up!" Veronica sang as she lifted Regan's blanket and tickled her feet.

What did I do to deserve this? Regan wondered futilely as she struggled to open her eyes. No matter how hard she tried to become a morning person, Regan had never been able to turn herself into one of those early risers who bound out of bed with glee. I should get a job working the night shift somewhere, she thought.

"I'm so glad we didn't stay in the casino for very long last night. Coming up here and reading in bed was such a joy, although I stayed up later than I wanted to with your mother's book. You had already fallen asleep, Regan, and I had to force myself to turn out the light at one o'clock. I can't wait to tell your mother that when I finally meet her."

"Oh, that's nice, Veronica. She's always glad to hear people like her books." Regan rolled over, pulled the covers around her and contemplated how wonderful it would be to sleep for another hour or two. "What time is it?"

"Seven-thirty. We have to go down, have breakfast and be at the beauty parlor by nine o'clock."

"You're not going to exercise class this morning?"

"No time. We're having the works done today and then have to get ready for our soiree."

Regan sat up on her elbows. "We?"

"Of course. I've signed us each up for a manicure, pedicure, anti-aging facial, massage, seaweed treatment, blow-dry and a makeup application."

"Are you sure we'll be out of there by the time we get to New

York?" Regan asked as her feet hit the floor. But she admitted to herself that it certainly sounded better than going to any more financial or poetry seminars.

"Of course." Veronica zestily flung open the sliding glass door to the terrace and breathed in the salt air. Regan decided that the cilia in Veronica's nose got more of a workout than the bristles on an industrial-strength vacuum.

"They'll serve us lunch there," Veronica explained. "Unfortunately we'll have to forgo any lectures today. I suppose it goes with the territory of being a charming, beautiful hostess." Veronica walked out onto the deck singing, "What I did for love . . ."

Regan stared out at her as she stretched her legs and arms. Veronica is generous, she thought. She doesn't have to treat me to all that. It's going to cost her a fortune. Regan walked into the bathroom and looked at her reflection, complete with two dark circles under her eyes. I guess the anti-aging facial isn't coming a minute too soon.

"ARE YOU COMFORTABLE, Miss Reilly?" the young "aesthetician" with perfect skin and makeup asked Regan as she finished wrapping her body in a plastic film and thermal blankets.

About as comfortable as one can get with slimy smelly seaweed covering just about every inch of available skin, Regan thought. "Yes, I'm fine."

"That's good because anyone who gets claustrophobic can really get bothered by this."

Now she tells me.

"But you're going to feel sooo good when this is over. All the dead skin cells will be washed away and the toxins will be flushed out of your system."

"That's what a woman at my table told me."

"Who's that?"

"Immaculata Buttacavola."

"Oh yes, she was in here the other day. Lovely woman. She enjoys talking about her family."

"I know."

"As a matter of fact, she'll be back this afternoon to get her hair done. Said she's going to some party tonight. I suppose that must be yours."

"Yes."

"Lovely," she said in that soft whispery voice that beautifiers were trained to use in these darkened self-improvement tombs. "Relax. Enjoy. I'll be right outside if you need me. In a half hour we'll unwrap you and you'll take a shower before the second part of the treatment." She shut the door reverentially and Regan closed her eyes.

Minutes passed and Regan realized that she couldn't relax. Thoughts of Athena and her family once again consumed her. Athena's body found under a pile of leaves, still and lifeless. Penelope being poisoned. Questions about Cameron Hardwick. Regan squirmed as the blanket heated up and she realized how limited her ability for movement was. It paralleled the way she felt about her work on the case. Not much she could do in the middle of the ocean. She was stifled. Damn it! I'm wasting my time here, she thought as sweat seemed to ooze from every pore.

The body mask was becoming too warm. It made her feel wet and soggy. She tried to move her arms but they were pinned to her sides by the heavy blankets.

An instant of sheer blind panic seized Regan as she imagined Athena's body rotting in the woods adjacent to Llewellyn Hall, covered by dank-smelling muddy leaves.

"Miss. Missssss," she called.

IT WAS 3 P.M. BY the time Regan and Veronica got back to the suite.

A coiffed, manicured, massaged, made-up Regan said, "Thank you, Veronica. After a bad start, that turned out to be really nice."

"Ah well, a little primping is good for the soul, don't you think? I'm sorry the seaweed wrap didn't work for you, dear. When I was in it I just pretended it was Sir Gilbert holding me tight. Naturally I didn't want it to end." Veronica looked in the mirror over her dresser and fluffed her hair. "Have you ever been in love, Regan?"

"Once in the seventh grade."

Veronica chuckled. "No, I mean really."

"I've had a few false starts. Who knows?" Regan shrugged her shoulders and inspected her nails, now covered with a shade called ravishing red. Are these too bright? she wondered. Maybe I should have gone with perilous plum or sexy strawberry. Who sits around and thinks up those names?

"When you are," Veronica continued, "it will change your life. You will just know it's right. I suppose you have to kiss a lot of frogs before you find your prince."

"Well, I've kissed a lot of princes who've turned into frogs," Regan muttered.

"Regan, I just hope you end up with someone like Sir Gilbert. I know I tend to go on a bit too much about him, but he was and always will be the love of my life."

Regan sat down on the bed next to her. "It certainly seems like it."

"Oh, dear, I was a bit spinsterish when I met him. And everyone thought I was crazy to spend so much time with a man so old. But he had such a young spirit. He made me feel so special and loved. Being in his presence was like coming home. Some people thought I was with him because of his money." Veronica's voice rose. "But it wasn't true. He wanted to marry me quickly so that I'd be taken care of if anything happened to him. I thought it was too soon, but he insisted." Veronica sighed. "Those two weeks were the best of my life. And I've never found anyone who could replace him. But"—Veronica jumped up—"that doesn't mean I can't keep trying, does it, Regan?" She clapped her hands. "We have got to get a party going here. The bartender and waiter will be arriving at four o'clock to set up, and we have to be ready by then. And I think it would be a jolly good idea to break out a bottle of champagne to drink while we're getting dressed. What do you say, Regan?"

"Why not?"

"Indeed why not?" Veronica headed for the refrigerator. "After all, you only live once, right?"

"Right."

"Oh, Regan, this is such good fun and we only have one full day left. I can't help getting excited about meeting my niece and her children, but in a way I hate to see our journey end."

AT FIVE O'CLOCK the Camelot Suite had the look of pre-party anticipation. Fresh flowers had been placed at strategic points around the room, a cheese board and crudités were set out on the cocktail table and the bartender was at his post cutting up lemons and limes. Out on the terrace the waiter was at a mini-oven organizing the trays of hot hors d'oeuvres. The late-afternoon sun was gleaming off the water as the *Queen Guinevere* moved majestically on its course to New York.

"We have enough food here for an army," Regan commented as she helped herself to a carrot stick.

"Ah, well, it's always better to have too much than not enough," Veronica said airily.

So what was the problem at your party at Llewellyn Hall last week? Regan thought as there was a knock at the door. I bet it's Robin Leach.

"Coming," Veronica sang as she checked herself in the mirror one last time, strolled to the door and with a sweeping gesture opened it as if she were parting the Pearly Gates. Standing there was not their first guest but the gawky young steward, shifting his weight from one foot to the other.

"I have an envelope for Miss Reilly."

"Thank you, my dear. Would you like to come in for a drink?"

"Sorry, ma'am, I would love to, but I'm on duty."

"Well, if you get a break, do pop in. Who knows how long our party will last?"

"Splendid."

Regan hurried down the steps and took the envelope from Veronica's hands. "It must be the rest of the faxes from Greece. I'll just take a quick look." Standing in the foyer, with Veronica looking over her shoulder, Regan ripped it open and pulled out its contents. On the first page was a picture of Athena with her aunt, Helen's three children, and their governess. The caption read, "Minutes before her death, Helen Carvelous posed on the beach at Skoulis for what was to be the last picture ever taken with her children."

"Why, that's Val."

"What are you talking about, Veronica?"

"Next to the dark-haired girl."

"Next to Athena?"

"Oh, that's right. That is Athena. Poor girl. Well, that's Val standing right next to her. I was going through one of Philip's Saint Polycarp's yearbooks from about ten years ago and came across her picture. It was the first year she taught there. She looked exactly like that."

Regan felt adrenaline shoot through her body. Stay calm, she thought. Val had never admitted to knowing Athena.

"But Veronica, this is such a grainy picture. It's been reproduced on fax paper. And back then, everyone wore their hair this way. Look, it identifies her as Mary V. Cook." Is she thinking this way because she's already had three glasses of champagne? Regan thought.

"Well then, she's what you would call a dead ringer for her. And what does the *V* stand for?" Veronica added before she dismissed the subject and reached over to answer the second knock at the door. Cameron Hardwick filled the doorway.

"Hello, ladies."

"Our first guest," Veronica cried. "Do come in."

"Hi, Cameron," Regan said as she stuffed the faxes back into the envelope. Opening the top drawer of the dresser, she dropped it inside as she silently wished she had time to study it now. I won't be able to get back to it until after dinner, she thought anxiously.

"Look, Regan, Cameron brought us a box of chocolates. Isn't that thoughtful?"

"Oh yes, how nice," Regan said as she remembered the last time a guy had presented her with chocolates. An old boyfriend from New York, he'd flown to Los Angeles for a business meeting. Only later did she learn that the chocolates were a giveaway to first-class passengers on TransAmerica Airlines.

Everyone knows there are people who recycle wedding gifts, Regan thought as she plucked what she hoped was a chocolate-covered caramel from the corner pocket of Cameron's offering and popped it in her mouth. Why not chocolates? But as she chewed the creamy confection, a nervous pit grew in her stomach. Val and Cameron have both been placed in Greece and neither one of them has owned up to it. Why? But Veronica could be wrong. So could Violet. I'm going to have to find out what town Violet Cohn was in, Regan thought. And I can't wait to call Livingston. Of course, even if Val and Cameron were both there, that still doesn't mean they did anything wrong.

She looked out at the deck where the waiter was pulling a tray of hors d'oeuvres from the oven, then took a deep breath as she remembered that Val had also been at Llewellyn Hall when Penelope was poisoned.

"Boy, this place is swank," Mario's voice boomed as he and Immaculata caught their first glimpse of the Camelot Suite. "Honey, if we ever win the lottery, we'll have to take another cruise and book this suite."

"First we have to put some money away for the children's educations, Mario. But then we could take the whole family away with us. Wouldn't that be great?" Immaculata's eyes sparkled at the prospect.

Regan joined them. "You could have the rest of the family stay in the suite across the hall, then you'd have the whole area to yourself. So how about that, Mario?"

Mario laughed as he put his arm around Immaculata. "Now don't go giving my wife ideas. So there's just one other suite up here, huh?"

"Yes, and it's empty for this crossing. We should have gotten the key and had a suite-to-suite party," Regan said, trying to get into the mode of cocktail-party chatter. "Then Veronica could have invited everyone on board."

"I think she already did," Dale added from the doorway, a smiling Kenneth behind him. "There were a number of people waiting for the elevator."

"I'll get our drinks before the bar gets too crowded. What would you like, honey?" Mario asked Immaculata.

"Now let's see," Immaculata began, "I already had one of the special drinks of the day and that had rum in it. I don't really feel like having a rum drink, but maybe I should since that's what I started with and it's not a good idea to mix. Oh, but look! They have champagne and—"

"Come with me to the bar while you make up your mind." Mario turned to Regan and Dale. "Excuse us."

"This place is unbelievable," Dale said, looking around as Kenneth stepped over to the bar.

"Isn't it?" Regan agreed as she took a sip of her champagne and noticed Hardwick slip out onto the terrace and stand at the railing, his back to the others.

"Regan, I love the way they did your hair," Kenneth said as he handed Dale a Scotch. "A little too much spray, but they always seem to do that."

"Kenneth and I can never leave our jobs at home," Dale smiled. "While I'm checking out the furniture, he's looking at people's hair and thinking she could use a body wave, he could use a better color job . . ."

"Or he could use hair, she could use a comb," Kenneth chimed in. "Regan, we've set it up with Veronica to meet you up here Saturday morning at four A.M. We're going to have champagne and I'm going to do a comb-out on Veronica's hair. She wants to look great to meet her nieces. We want to be downstairs by five so that we can be on the deck when we sail into New York and past the Statue of Liberty."

"Four A.M.?" Regan echoed.

"It's a tradition you don't want to miss. We'll probably just stay up all night partying. Why don't you join us?" Dale asked.

"Thanks, guys, but I think I'll grab a few hours of sleep first," Regan commented.

Within a half hour the party was in full swing. Sylvie came in with Milton and Violet. As Regan greeted them she noticed that Sylvie had the look of someone who had scored a big one, obviously pleased with the chance to impress Milton and his disdainful sister.

"Um-hmmm," Violet said as she surveyed the surroundings with a critical eye. "Very nice. Oh, Milton, there's that rude young man. I don't know whether we should stay."

Regan realized that Violet was staring out at Cameron Hardwick as Sylvie's face became crestfallen.

Regan tucked her arm under Violet's and said, "Please stay. There are so many interesting people here. Lady Exner tells me that you met Cameron in Greece."

"Absolutely. He waited on us in 1981, the year my dear Bruce died."

As Regan escorted her to the bar she said casually, "On my next trip, I'm going to Greece. What town were you in?"

Without blinking an eye, Violet flatly declared, "Skoulis."

"No. No. No. Don't be silly, Mr. Gray. I will not allow it," Veronica was insistent.

"But it will only take a few minutes to get this place in order. You start down to dinner and I'll follow in a few minutes."

"No, you have done too much for us already. It's past seven-thirty and we're already late. The steward is going to come in and do the rest of the tidying up while we're at dinner." Veronica opened the door and started walking out. "The party was smashing, wasn't it?"

As Gavin reluctantly followed her, he agreed, "It was absolutely wonderful. And that's why I just wanted everything to be perfect for you when you came back to your room."

Regan pulled the door shut and as she walked down the hallway thought that he sounded as though he were pleading for his life.

Friday, June 26, 1992

I CAN'T WAIT any longer, Regan thought frantically as she crept out of bed. She peered over at Veronica, who appeared to be sleeping soundly. The clock next to the bed read 4:30. Which meant it was 8:30 A.M. in Oxford.

Regan tiptoed into the bathroom, shut the door and picked up the phone on the wall.

Five minutes later she was speaking with Superintendent Livingston.

"I'm so glad I caught you in," she whispered as she told him about Veronica's belief that Val was the governess in the picture with Athena and her aunt and children.

Livingston looked down at the papers on his desk and shuffled through them until he found the picture in question. Holding it up, he studied it. "Could be," he said. "Hard to be certain, of course. The photo is rather grainy. She's identified as Mary V. Cook. I'll stop over at Saint Polycarp's today and look into her employment records."

"And another thing," Regan continued, "there's an American guy on board who sits at our table and to me his background doesn't gel. An older woman I've met insists he waited on her in Skoulis, Greece, eleven years ago. It's just a hunch, but could you check with the police in Greece? See if his name came up at all during the investigation. Maybe he was questioned if he worked in the town. Skoulis is not that big."

"I'd be happy to. What's his name?"

"Cameron Hardwick."

Oxford

As LIVINGSTON DROVE once again up the road to St. Polycarp's, he reviewed the case in his mind. If indeed Valerie Twyler had been the governess, why was she hiding it? Was the burglary of Helen Carvelous's home which led to murder an inside job? What about this chap named Cameron Hardwick? Livingston had called Greece and asked them to pull out the files on the Carvelous murder investigation.

It was 9:05 A.M. when he pulled into the parking lot. As expected, Reginald Crane, the headmaster, was already at his desk.

"Nigel, this is the second visit this week." Crane reached over and shook his hand. "Please sit down. What can I do for you this time?"

Livingston sat back in his chair and took a deep breath. He had to be careful. Her reputation was at stake. "Miss Valerie Twyler. Could you please get out her records?"

Without hesitation Crane got up and walked over to his battered-looking cabinet. "I assume I can't ask why you're interested in Val Twyler."

"Just checking some facts," Nigel replied as he pulled his notebook out of his pocket.

Tossing the file on his desk, Crane sat back down and opened it. He explained that the first page was the notes he had taken when he interviewed her for the position.

"When was that?" Livingston asked.

"April 23, 1982."

Livingston felt energy dart through his body. That was the

same day Athena Popolous disappeared. "Where was Twyler working at the time?"

"A school about seventy-five miles west of here. A place called Pearsons Hall."

"Did she ever list any references from Greece or mention working there as a governess?"

Crane flipped through his papers. "No, she didn't."

"Do you know if she was ever married?"

"Apparently she had been divorced the year before she came here. She even went back to using her maiden name."

"What was her married name?"

"Cook."

The Inspector stood up. "Exactly where is Pearsons Hall?"

At Sea

WHEN SHE TIPTOED back to bed after talking to Livingston, Regan tossed and turned. Sleep was out of the question. Her mind would not stop racing. Violet Cohn. She had a mind like a steel trap. I'd lay odds that she's right, Regan thought. Cameron Hardwick had been her waiter in Skoulis. If Val had been a governess there, maybe she'd met Cameron in town. Maybe she had tipped him off about the jewelry. The antique jewelry, in his own words, "the only jewelry worth having."

Regan lay on her side and hugged the pillow, once again staring out at the terrace where Cameron had spent most of the evening. If Val and Cameron were somehow involved, was there a connection to Athena's death? And what was Hardwick doing on this ship?

Oxford

INSPECTOR LIVINGSTON DROVE most of the seventy-five miles to Pearsons Hall barely noticing the tranquil English countryside.

It was 11:30 A.M. when he found himself seated in another office, this time waiting for the headmistress, Margaret Heslop, to return from a meeting down the hall. At a quarter to twelve the door flew open and with a cane a woman pushed it wide as she wheeled herself in.

Livingston jumped up. "Can I be of help?"

"Good Lord no, I've been managing this since the war," she said heartily. A sixtyish matron with a pleasant face and gray hair pulled back in a chignon, she settled herself opposite Livingston's chair and extended her hand. "Margaret Heslop."

"Nigel Livingston. I appreciate you seeing me on such short notice."

"I knew it must be important. Otherwise you wouldn't have come all the way from Oxford." And then, with an efficient air, she added, "Tell me your business."

"I need to discuss the background of Valerie Twyler."

"Valerie Twyler?" Heslop sounded puzzled.

"Her married name was Cook."

"Of course." The headmistress's face clouded as she shook her head. "I never think of her as Twyler. She went back to her maiden name after divorcing a chap in town."

"I understand she also was referred to as Mary for most of the time she taught here." For the second time that morning Livingston found himself toying with his pen and notebook.

"All of the time, actually," Heslop replied.

"Right. Do you know if she ever spent any of her summers working as a governess in Greece?"

"She most certainly did, and that was the start of her troubles." Heslop rolled her wheelchair over to her file cabinet and pulled out a folder marked "Mary V. Cook."

"What do you mean, troubles?" Livingston asked quickly.

"Isn't that why you're here?" Heslop asked as she snapped the drawer shut and opened the file at her desk. "She was getting a divorce from her husband and wanted to get away for the summer. She worked for a family in Greece where, as I'm sure you know, there was a tragedy. A woman walked in on a burglary and was murdered. Since Mary was the only one living there who was not a family member, she was questioned extensively. When she came back here for the fall term, the police kept showing up and asking her questions. We weren't too happy about it. It got to be a bit disruptive, embarrassing and all. I gather they couldn't prove anything. Finally there was an opening at Saint Polycarp's and she grabbed the chance to get away. She interviewed for the job and I understand has been there ever since. I even heard she's getting married."

"Yes, she is."

"Well, I hope he fares better than Malcolm Cook did in that situation. She could be a rather difficult woman. An excellent teacher but not very personable."

No wonder she never wanted to admit knowing Athena, Livingston thought. It made perfect sense that she wanted to start a new life for herself. And even if she was interviewed the day Athena disappeared, it might be totally irrelevant. He had seen those incongruous coincidences where people happened to be in the wrong place at the wrong time.

Livingston thanked Margaret Heslop for her time and got up to leave, promising not to hesitate to call if he needed any more questions answered.

At the staircase that went down to the carpark he hesitated, pausing a moment to soak up the momentary bout of sunlight that crept from behind the clouds while he reflected on what he had just heard.

"Oh dear, now where did I park that darn thing?"

Livingston looked over at an older woman whom he guessed to be about seventy and smiled.

"My husband always gets a bit ratty because I can never remember where I parked the car. He has trouble walking, so I drop him off at the door and then go park it. They're having a crafts fair in the auditorium today. Some lovely things. You might want to have a look."

Trying to help, Livingston asked, "What kind of car do you have?"

"It's a blue Austin and it's been giving us a good deal of trouble lately. We've been calling our blue Austin our bad apple." She cackled to herself. "Oh, thank you, now I see it," she said as she grabbed hold of the railing and negotiated her way down the steps.

Blue Austin. Bad Apple. B.A. Livingston flipped through his notebook and looked up exactly what had been written on the matchbook found in Athena Popolous's pocket. "B.A. 315."

Turning on his heel he hurried back inside. "I'm taking you up on your offer sooner than you think," he told the surprised headmistress. "Did you by any chance keep a record of faculty automobiles?"

"Of course. Faculty members all get stickers for the carpark."

"What kind of car did Valerie—er—Mrs. Cook drive when she was here?"

"Now let's see. Her file's right here. Ah yes, it was a blue Austin."

"What was the license number?" Livingston asked tightly.

"Three-one-five-seven-six-four."

"You've been most helpful."

Valerie Twyler, or Mary V. Cook, had known Athena Popolous in Greece, Livingston thought as he got into his car. For some reason Athena had written down part of Val's license plate. Athena disappeared the day Val had her interview in Oxford. And Val had also accused Veronica of trying to poison Penelope Atwater, an idea that instinctively he found hard to believe. Regan Reilly had certainly disputed the notion. Another thing. Val's upcoming marriage to Philip Whitcomb didn't make sense. They seemed like oil and water. Was she marrying him because he was the probable heir to Lady Exner and her millions? If she indeed had tried to poison Penelope Atwater, there was no telling what she had planned next. And how soon. A sense of urgency made him lean his foot on the accelerator as he hurried back to Oxford.

At Sea

CAMERON HARDWICK WAS having a sleepless night. In his mind he kept going over and over his plan. He mentally visualized the stateroom. If the old bag woke up when he was getting rid of Reilly, it would be too risky. He looked over at the vial of knockout drops he had on his dresser. They were the kind that worked over several hours. He'd drop them into her drink tonight and by ten or eleven at the latest, Exner's chin would be impaled on her chest. After her party last night, it wouldn't be surprising if she seemed exhausted. By the time he stole into the suite she'd be in never-never land. He smiled to himself.

Reilly. He'd love to sweeten her drink, but it was much too hazardous. He could feel strange vibes coming from her. She'd never let him get that close. And even if she did, if she started getting exceptionally sleepy, an alarm would sound in her head. No, he was hoping to use the element of surprise in her case. If she was asleep when he got inside, he'd have the extra few seconds he needed. If not, he knew he could get to her before she could reach for the phone. He'd checked. The phone in the living room was on a table in back of the sofa bed, too far away to grab before he got to her. If she tried to yell, it wouldn't do her any good. What was that line? If a tree falls in a forest and no one is there, does it make a sound?

Hardwick glanced at the clock. Six A.M. I may as well get up, he thought. It's going to be an interesting day. And the weather was even supposed to cooperate. A good omen. Overcast skies were predicted for tonight. As he turned on the shower, the smell of heavily chlorinated water stung his nostrils. How can people who work on this ship stand bathing in this water week in and week out? he thought. The steward. Let's hope he won't try to get in the way tonight. By one o'clock in the morning he'd hopefully be passed out at his station, anesthetized by Dr. Jack Daniels. I'll get past him, do my business and come back down here and wait. For land, freedom and the big payment.

FOR SOME REASON, I'm jumpy today and worried about Veronica, Regan thought as she and Veronica dressed. They had slept later than usual. Regan had finally fallen asleep after 5 A.M. and Veronica's perpetual state of motion was beginning to catch up with her. She had decided to skip the Sit-and-Be-Fit class.

"It's all right, Regan," Veronica proclaimed. "I really do feel quite well. Today will be a good day for relaxing, regrouping, saying good-bye to our new friends and preparing for the second part of my adventure, which begins tomorrow."

"What, no seminars at all?" Regan asked.

"I really don't think I need to hear about financial planning again. Philip has someone taking care of all that for me. As for the psychic, well, I'd rather have a personal session with one in New York. I hear there are several good ones who work in restaurants. They come around to your table. I'll have to bring my nieces." Veronica sat down to the breakfast tray. "I'm so glad we decided to order room service today. And after this we can take it easy down on the Lido Deck, as we did the other afternoon."

"That's a good idea," Regan said. There was a knock. She put down her own coffee cup. "Now who might that be?" she asked as she went to open the door.

A nervous-looking Gabby Gavin stood in front of her. "Is everything all right?" he asked. "I was worried when Lady Exner didn't show up for exercise class this morning."

"Yes, yes, everything's fine," Veronica called from the living room. "Today is a day to unwind. Come in, Mr. Gray."

As he walked past her Regan thought he seemed to have aged in the last couple of days.

"I'd like to escort you to all the activities today, Lady Exner. It's such a pleasure being in your company, and this is our last day. Regan, maybe you'd like to be on your own."

"Thank you, Gavin, but today Veronica and I are just going to relax down on the Lido Deck. Right, Veronica?"

"Absolutely. Why don't you join us? It's a long time since such a handsome gentleman has desired my presence."

There goes the flirt in Veronica, Regan thought. I wonder if she'll ever write a poem about Gabby.

"OH, MARIO, I can't wait," Immaculata rejoiced as she put on her eye makeup. "What time will we go up there?"

"The steward said anytime after ten," Mario answered as he tied the laces of his sneakers. "We'll have our own private party in one of the two best suites on the ship. Right now I'm just dying for some breakfast."

Her second coat of mascara in place, Immaculata zipped closed her makeup bag. "I've got my special black negligee. Aren't we lucky there's no one staying in that suite and the steward is so nice?"

"Honey, for a price anybody is nice."

"I know, but he could still get in trouble."

"Yeah, well, I told him, it's like a second honeymoon for us and we could never afford to stay in a place like that. No one will ever know, and he gets a couple hundred bucks extra spending money." Mario put his arms around Immaculata and gave her a hug. "We'll relive our wedding night."

Immaculata looked puzzled. "But, Mario, don't you remember? You fell asleep on our wedding night."

Oxford

IT WAS AFTER 2 P.M. when Livingston got back to his office. Several messages were piled on his desk, the most important one from the authorities in Greece. He quickly called back and learned that Cameron Hardwick had indeed been questioned at the time of Helen Carvelous's death. He had been employed as a waiter at the local hotel. The week before the murder he had been one of the extra help hired for a large party at the Carvelous mansion. They had no forwarding address for him.

As Livingston hung up the phone he reflected on the fact that Twyler and Hardwick almost undoubtedly had known each other in Greece. Now Hardwick was traveling on the *Queen Guinevere*. Five minutes later he was speaking to an agent at the Global Cruise Line's headquarters in London. After identifying himself, he asked, "Do you have an address for a Cameron Hardwick who is now sailing for New York on the *Queen Guinevere*?"

"Certainly should have. One moment, sir." The woman's voice sounded dignified but friendly.

As Livingston waited he wondered when he would be able to grab a sandwich. He hadn't eaten anything since early that morning.

The dignified voice began talking again. "All right then. I have on the list here a Cameron Hardwick who gave us a post office box in New York City."

"That's it?"

"Yes, sir. Sorry."

Livingston was about to hang up when he had a thought.

"Did he give any local phone number for where he could be reached before he boarded the ship?"

"Actually he did. We always ask for a number where we can contact our passengers before sailing in case there is any sort of delay."

Livingston jotted down the number, which had a Highgate exchange. Highgate was only thirty miles from Oxford. "Thank you." Quickly he dialed and anxiously waited as the phone rang six or seven times. Finally it was answered by what sounded like an older man. "Barleyneck Inn. Mason Hicks, at your service. Yes, yes. Can I help you? Oh my. Please hold on."

Livingston looked at the receiver with a quizzical look. "I'm holding." He listened as the voice at the other end apologized to someone who presumably was registering a complaint.

"Oh my, your tea wasn't hot, was it? So sorry. Have a seat. We'll get you another pot straightaway. Yes, yes. Have a seat. Have a seat—can I help you?"

Livingston drummed his fingers on the desk.

"Can I help you?" the voice repeated.

Livingston sat up in his chair as he introduced himself. "I need to know if there is a Cameron Hardwick there, or has he been there?"

"Cameron Hardwick. Yes."

"Yes?" Livingston sounded surprised.

"Yes. Yes, he checked out at the beginning of the week. Hold on a moment, please.—Hello, it's lovely to have you back. Sign the book, please.—Hello. Yes. So sorry. Cameron Hardwick checked out on Monday morning. A quiet chap. Very neat. Always borrowing the ironing board." A laugh resembling a wheeze traveled through the telephone wires.

"He's been there before?"

"Oh yes, yes. Oh-oh, hold on a moment."

Livingston waited impatiently as the clerk rang a bell and called for a porter. When he got back on, Livingston asked for the address of the inn and how to get there. It'll take all day to get any information on the phone, he thought to himself. After giving him the directions, the clerk said to Livingston, "Shall I reserve a room for you? We've got quite a nice one facing the stream."

"No, but I will stop by this afternoon, if you will be there."

"Yes, yes, of course. We serve tea and scones at four. My wife makes homemade jam. Oh-oh, hold on a moment."

"That's all right," Livingston yelled into the phone before the voice went away. "I'll see you later." He winced as he hung up. I'm getting a bit cranky, he thought. I need a real meal, but not before I ring Valerie Twyler. There was no answer at her home, so he decided to try Llewellyn Hall. The maid answered.

"She and Philip have gone off to Bath for the day with some of the students who arrived for the summer program. They won't be back till tonight around half ten or eleven. I'm here alone waiting hand and foot on Penelope."

"How is she feeling?" Livingston asked.

"Her appetite's back," she said flatly.

"I see."

"I'm not getting any younger, and all those trips up and down the stairs. 'More tea, please. Get me some crackers. Would you mind making me some soup?' You'd think all of a sudden that she owned the place. When Lady Exner gets back I'm asking for a raise."

"Right." Livingston tried to sound sympathetic. "I'll try to reach Miss Twyler this evening."

"Whatever you'd like. I'll be home by then, soaking my poor feet, parked in front of the telly. 'Bye."

Livingston was relieved to hear the receiver click in his ear. He glanced at his watch. Two forty-five. Time for a quick plowman's lunch and a pot of tea at the pub across the street and then I'm off to the Barleyneck Inn, he thought. He had a feeling that the proprietor of the hotel would be only too happy to chat him up about Cameron Hardwick. As he walked out of the station house he only wished he didn't have to wait until that night to question Valerie Twyler. His wife had hoped that he'd be able to be home that evening. But something told him that it shouldn't wait until morning. Oh well, he thought as he entered the darkened pub, I can always decide after my visit to the Barleyneck. Maybe after I get through with that bloke I'll be ready to call it a day.

THE BARLEYNECK INN was located at the end of a cul-de-sac in a farming village. As Livingston turned down the street he paused to allow a few free-roaming sheep to cross the road. They stared at him with bored expressions as they made no attempt to hasten their progress, the only outward sign of their heartbeat being an occasional "baaaa." "Hurry up," Livingston muttered to himself, "before you find yourself lying in front of my fireplace."

Pulling into the driveway, Livingston found a small country inn, charming in a Victorian sense, nestled below large oak trees. Inside, the atmosphere was pleasant. Floral draperies and wallpaper in the community room offset the rich dark paneling in the foyer. An old man whom Livingston guessed to be the one he had spoken to sat at a large antique desk urging a young couple to be sure and come again. Weathered skin was topped by thinning gray hair. Bifocals rested on his amiable-looking nose. He looks as if he's been here since the Reformation, Livingston thought.

"I hope everything was to your liking."

"Splendid," the young woman answered quickly as she tapped her foot impatiently.

"Yes, yes. Traveling around a bit, are you?"

"We're headed back to Australia in a couple of days," the thirtyish-looking man replied as he put his credit card back in his wallet. "Well, thank you."

"I've always wanted to go to Australia but never quite made it. Where in Australia are you from?"

"Melbourne."

"Yes, yes. Maybe I'll get there someday, but—"

"Excuse me," Livingston interrupted as the young couple looked at him gratefully and grabbed their suitcases. "If you don't mind, I'd like to have a word with you."

"Yes. Certainly. 'Bye now," the innkeeper called to the departing duo, who were now halfway out the door.

"I'm Inspector Livingston. I spoke with you this morning."

"Indeed. You're the one who wants to know about Cameron Hardwick. I've been thinking about him since you called. A nice enough chap, I suppose. An American. But picky, picky, picky."

"Do you think we could talk about this in private?" Livingston asked even as he acknowledged that there seemed to be no one else around. From the sound of all the activity during the phone call this morning, you would have thought it was the Ritz.

"Certainly. By the way, I'm Mason Hicks." The man's look of curiosity was hearty. "Now let me summon my helper so he can man the desk while we go into my private office." He hit a circular bell at his desk three times. "I should have called him to carry their suitcases out," he added as he pointed his finger in the direction of the front door and then, temporarily exasperated, hit the bell twice again.

A timid-looking oldster appeared from around the corner. The Palace Guard, Livingston thought.

"Rodney, do you think you can man the desk? We have a great emergency here, yes yes," Hicks declared.

Rodney squared his shoulders as he took command. "Er, would you like some tea first?" he asked politely.

"No, thank you," Livingston replied.

Hicks led him into a tiny musty-smelling office whose walls abounded with pictures of hounds leaping over fences.

"I don't want to keep you," Livingston began as he sat down on a red leather chair squeezed between a statue of a dalmatian and the draperies.

"Take your time, take your time, um-hmmm, yes," Hicks

said as he folded his hands in front of him, clearly enjoying the excitement only a police officer's presence can engender. "So you're doing an investigation of Cameron Hardwick, eh?"

"Routine questioning, really," Livingston replied. He cleared his throat. "Over the phone you indicated that Cameron Hardwick is a frequent guest."

"We love those kind." Hicks's eyes crinkled as he smiled and leaned forward.

"Right," Livingston replied. "How often would you say he visits?"

"A couple of times a year maybe. Good-looking fellow in a brooding way. He has a lady friend who frequently comes by and stays with him." Hicks fired a huge suggestive wink.

Livingston looked up from his ever-present notebook. "Can you describe her?"

"Ohhh, late thirties, I suppose. Brown hair. Attractive enough in a plain sort of way. A bit prim. You wouldn't think she's the type to carry on an affair, but you know what, I think she's married!" As Hicks's eyes lit up, he pushed his elbow out in a nudge-nudge, wink-wink motion and shook his head up and down.

"Do you by any chance know her name?"

"I believe he always calls her Mary. She never gave a surname. He always books the reservation. We have ten beautiful rooms, but he always likes to stay in the same one, every time. It has its own private bath. Once it wasn't available and he got a bit nasty—"

"I see, I see," Livingston interrupted. "When was the last time you saw his lady friend?"

"A day or two before he left. That was last weekend. She came by on Saturday morning and they had tea sent up to the room. He likes his privacy and everything has to be just so. His eggs have to be cooked a certain way, his bacon must be crisp . . . He jogs every day. Told me if he didn't he'd go crazy."

"It sounds like you remember quite a bit about him," Livingston remarked.

"Well, he's been coming here for the past ten years," Hicks exclaimed.

"Ten years?" Livingston asked.

"Yes, yes. He came in and was the first guest to stay in the room overlooking the stream after it had been redone. The girl joined him that night. They were both very pleased with the accommodations and have been coming back ever since. My wife and I decided it reminds us of the movie *Same Time Next Year*. Did you ever see that?"

"Yes, enjoyable film," Livingston replied.

"Yes, yes. It makes one wonder what they have to hide."

"It certainly does," Livingston answered as he got up and realized it was going to be a long evening until he got the opportunity to question Valerie Twyler, also known as Mary Cook.

At Sea

IT WAS THE most relaxed day of the crossing. Veronica was clearly preserving her energy for her newfound relatives. Regan in a deck chair on one side, Gabby Gavin on the other, Veronica held court with passersby but did not at any time spring to her feet. Gavin fussed incessantly over her. First he was afraid the sun would burn her. Didn't she have a sunblock lotion he could fetch for her from the suite? Veronica dived into her tote bag and triumphantly yanked out a sunblock 32—maximum protection.

"They say not a ray will damage your skin, not even if you're sunbathing on the equator," she chortled.

Gavin looked glum.

They did not go into the dining room but had the buffet lunch near the pool. Regan brought Veronica a club sandwich and a margarita with a little paper umbrella bobbing among the ice cubes.

Veronica extricated the umbrella and tossed it into her bag. "That's for my scrapbook. It will always remind me of this special day with you, dear Mr. Gray."

"Are you sure you're not chilled by the wind?" he asked anxiously. "Let me go get a sweater for you."

"No need," Veronica proclaimed as she yanked a shawl out of her seemingly bottomless tote bag. "Dear Regan thinks of everything."

Regan thought she detected hostility in the glance Gabby threw at her.

"And now I must complete the book of my favorite author.

Mr. Gray, did you know that Regan's mother is Nora Regan Reilly, the famous suspense writer?"

Gabby had a twisted, sadistic look on his face. Alarmed, Regan noticed her mother and father were just coming around the side of the pool. She was sure Gabby spotted them at the same moment. He clamped his lips as Nora whirled around and fled back into the lounge, a resigned-looking Luke in her wake.

At 4 P.M. Regan and Veronica started upstairs to begin packing before dinner.

"As Regan has pointed out, it would be so much better if we get most of it out of the way before dinner, since the bags have to be out in the hallway before we retire." Veronica waved the tote bag at Gavin. "Au 'voir."

"Au 'voir, my ass," Gavin muttered under his breath.

Oxford

THERE WAS NOTHING he could do except wait out the return of Val and Philip. Livingston decided he might as well go home and have a decent dinner with the family. His wife, Maude, always sensitive to his moods, observed quietly, "Something brewing, I gather. I was sure I'd be putting the lamb in the fridge for you."

He was attacking it vigorously. "It would be a shame not to have it fresh and hot. I do have to go out later."

"Oh, Daddy," Davina wailed. "I was hoping you could drive me and Elizabeth and Courtney and Laura to cinema."

"Not tonight, I'm afraid."

"But we're all planning to go." Davina looked horrified. "It's important."

"I'd like to think that my appointment is important too," Livingston said dryly. "Where are Elizabeth's and Courtney's and Laura's fathers tonight?"

"All very busy. Maybe you could—"

"Davina, let your father enjoy his dinner in peace," Maude ordered.

Peace. Livingston looked at Davina with irritated affection. Since the moment they'd carried her home from hospital, peace had been a rare commodity in this household.

Somehow that reminded him of Athena Popolous. From what he'd learned, she'd been at odds with her parents. Not that Davina was at odds, of course. But Athena had been only five years older than this pretty child who was looking at him with such indignant eyes. And Athena had been strangled and left to rot covered by brambles and underbrush.

He finished dinner quickly, gulped down a scalding cup of tea and pushed back from the table. "If you can get someone else's mother or father to pick you up, then I'll drop you off. But it has to be soon."

Davina jumped up and hugged him. "Thanks, Daddy."

"Right," Livingston replied as he watched her go pounding up the staircase so she could make the all-important phone calls in private.

There was always the chance that Val and Philip might get back early. In the meantime, he could visit with Penelope for a while. You never knew what tidbits she might be able to offer.

Giggling should be against the law, Livingston thought an hour later as he dropped off Davina and her friends at cinema. It was ten of eight. When he had phoned Llewellyn Hall, Emma Horne had promised to wait until he got there to admit him. "But don't make it any later than eight, please, sir, there's a program I want to watch tonight and I hate to miss the beginning. Turn it on even a minute or two late and you can't make head nor tail of it."

A rocket scientist, Livingston thought.

When he arrived, Emma was standing at the door, her large handbag firmly clasped in her arm.

"You know where her bedroom is. She's looking forward to seeing you. She's all fluffed up in bed, suffering for a visit. Better you than me." With the speed of light, Horne was backing her Land Rover out of the driveway, firing deadly pebbles into Philip's flower beds.

Livingston stood in the foyer a moment and looked around. If only the portraits of Sir Gilbert Exner's crusty ancestors could talk, he reflected as they glowered down at him. This house was a good three hundred years old. Forget the first two hundred ninety years. He'd love to know what had been going on here for the last ten. Not to mention the woods outside where Athena's body had been found.

He heard a greeting from upstairs. "I say, I'm up here," Penelope bellowed.

"I thought she was supposed to be half dead," Livingston muttered as he started up the stairs.

Penelope looked infinitely better than she had when he visited her in hospital. But that still wasn't saying very much. Livingston removed a sorry-looking teddy bear from her rocking chair, the only available seat in the room, and sat down, immediately forced to use his feet as brakes as the chair squeaked back and forth. The momentum finally subsided when Livingston got up, grabbed the chair and held it until it was still, and sat down again very warily. How many more years till my retirement? he wondered.

"You're looking well this evening, Miss Atwater," he lied.

"Oh, do you think so?" She flashed a smile that brought to mind that ridiculous American program "Mr. Ed."

Knowing that he was plunging into murky seas, he said, "I do hope you're feeling better."

Ten minutes later, feeling that he had had a crash course in gastrointestinal disasters, he was able to steer the conversation in the direction he had planned.

"I'm so sorry you missed the sailing. Are you planning to join Lady Exner in the States?"

The teeth disappeared, lost behind a thin, grim line. "The plans have not been defined."

Meaning, Livingston thought, that Lady Exner is not going to fly her over. He assumed a false heartiness. "I see. Well, you've had a narrow escape and perhaps a good rest will be better for you. Lady Exner will be back in a month's time and I'm sure you two will have a jolly time planning Philip and Val's wedding." He raised one eyebrow. "You don't seem very enthusiastic, Miss Atwater." He leaned forward confidentially, the rocking chair almost collapsing on top of him. "Are you?"

If he had opened the gates of a dam, the results could not

have been more satisfactory. Penelope Atwater virtually catapulted from her supine position on the fluffed-up pillows. "Enthusiastic? When the groom shows some enthusiasm, I'll show some. Lady Exner and I were shocked when they made their announcement last week. As Lady Exner said, there are two things in this world Philip cares about. His teaching position and his flowers."

"I understand he's been seeing Val for ten years," Livingston suggested mildly.

"That's the point." A conspiratorial whisper. "She always initiated their activities. Lady Exner and I think she's the one who brought about this engagement."

Livingston leaned forward, this time cautiously. "Are you suggesting . . . ?"

"A child? No, not that. But some kind of hold, yes."

PENELOPE ATWATER HAD given him plenty to think about, Livingston decided as he sat in the most comfortable club chair in the drawing room. Penelope had finally exhausted her pent-up reactions to the announcement of Val and Philip's impending nuptials. Actually her reaction made extremely good sense. Livingston mused that Philip obviously had a certain attraction for women, particularly starry-eyed young students, if the rumors were accurate. From what Penelope had observed in the past four years, if Philip had made a decision that it was time to marry, Val's aggressive personality would repel rather than intrigue him. As Penelope had said, "Val's very good at making herself useful, if you know what I mean. But some people are born bachelors, and Philip is one of them."

Livingston found himself realizing he might want to discuss that aspect further with Penelope. She had suddenly grown extemely tired and he had insisted on leaving her to her rest.

He thought longingly of his own bed and for a moment wondered if he should simply put off the questioning of Val Twyler until morning.

No. The certain instinct one of the old-timers called the hound-scent of the born detective was telling him to stay put.

Regan Reilly flashed into his mind. He hadn't called her today. There was nothing specific to report. His mind did arithmetic. Nine-thirty here. What time was it on the *Queen Guinevere*? He knew they turned the clock back an hour each night on the way to New York. Which would make it about five-thirty now. Miss Reilly would probably be at some cocktail party. He'd call her tomorrow at the number she'd given him in New Jersey. Maybe, after talking to Philip and Val, he'd have something substantial to report to her by then.

At Sea

THERE WAS SOMETHING about the last night on a ship, Regan thought. A certain regret at leaving people who had become pseudo-family members. She would probably never see Mario and Immaculata again, but she would remember them with affection. She would miss Veronica.

Cameron Hardwick was another piece of goods. She looked across the dinner table at him. For whatever reason, he was making an attempt to be particularly pleasant to Veronica, constantly engaging her in conversation. Sylvie was in an animated chat with Kenneth and Dale. Gabby looked as though he was about to burst into tears. He had indicated he would not be on another crossing for a while. She had the feeling that Gabby did not have much money behind him and that this ship represented luxury living. She found herself feeling sorry for him.

The dinner was particularly elaborate. Pâté, shrimp in pea pods, lobster bisque, veal medallions, trout almondine. Her mind blanked out at the rest of the menu. She longed for a plate of real Italian pasta. Angel hair with marinara sauce, a hunk of garlic bread, and I'm happy, she thought. Jeff always teased her about having the taste buds of a six-year-old.

Mario had insisted everyone order an after-dinner drink on him and Immaculata. "We've had such a great time sitting with you folks," he toasted the table.

Regan noticed that Immaculata was getting teary-eyed over her creme de menthe frappé. "Only the thought that Mario Junior and Roz and Mario the Third and Concepcione will be waiting to greet us at the pier makes this parting bearable."

Regan looked at Veronica. Cameron Hardwick's arm was around the back of Veronica's chair. Their brandy alexanders were side by side. Veronica's head was bobbing in agreement as he whispered in her ear.

Oxford

THE UNFORGETTABLE SOUND of the infamous St. Polycarp's van grinding to a halt in the driveway pulled Livingston awake. He had dozed off sometime after eleven and was startled to see that it was past midnight.

His limbs felt stiff. The evening had grown cooler and the room felt somewhat clammy.

The front door opened and slammed shut.

He was suddenly totally awake.

"Of all the absolutely appalling days I have ever passed, this, Philip, I assure you, has been uniquely abominable."

"I say, Val . . . I'm-I'm-I'm so sorry."

Livingston wondered if they'd even noticed his car. Perhaps not. It was parked around the turn of the driveway. He cleared his throat.

They did not hear him.

"First of all, how could you have forgotten to make the reservation for the new van when the last thing I did yesterday was to remind you?"

"But-but-but," Philip replied, "the bursar was taking his kiddies to a dental clinic in south London. He doesn't like to have them riding in the old van . . . the brakes, you know."

"And I'm supposed to ride in the piece of junk so they can get a discount on a few bloody fillings," Val shrieked. "We were taking students on a school outing, for God's sake. And why were we driving without a spare tire?"

"Careless of me, ho-ho-honeybunch," Philip whined. "Sorry-sorry . . . did cause a slight hiccup . . ."

Some lovebirds, Livingston thought. This time when he cleared his throat he was sure that Penelope could hear it upstairs.

Their shock at seeing him step from the drawing room was evident. Philip paled. "Has Penelope had a setback? Is she . . . ?"

Val seemed about to say something, then bit her lip as though guarding her reaction.

"No, no," Livingston said cordially. "I had quite a nice visit with Miss Atwater."

"Then . . ." Philip stopped.

Too polite to ask me what the devil I'm doing here, Livingston thought. "I just have a few questions for Miss Twyler."

"Certainly they'll keep until morning," Val snapped. "You can't possibly understand the sort of day I've had."

A cool one, Livingston thought, not for the first time. If she was nervous, she didn't show it. On the other hand, Philip looked apprehensive.

Val continued to stand in the foyer. "Please ask whatever you will and let me retire."

"Miss Twyler, are you also known as Mary V. Cook, and were you not a governess in the home of the aunt of Athena Popolous, a Mrs. Helen Carvelous, at the time Mrs. Carvelous was murdered?"

Philip gasped. "Val, when I told you about Athena—"

"Shut up," Val ordered.

"When you told what?" Livingston asked quietly.

"N-n-nothing," Philip stammered.

"Will you please accompany me to headquarters?" Livingston asked quietly. "We'll continue the questioning there."

They both knew it was not a request.

At Sea

THE WAITER CAME around offering more tea or coffee. Everyone seems anxious to get going, Regan thought. Typical at the end of a trip, when you've gotten temporarily close to fellow passengers but now were looking ahead.

Immaculata beamed. "I can't wait till tomorrow morning when we pass the Statue of Liberty. My grandmother's best friend, whose family came over here from Sicily, gave her pennies to the schoolchildren's fund so they could build a base for it. Can you believe they brought the statue all the way over here from France and for years didn't have the money for a base?"

Hardwick got up abruptly. "Good night, everyone."

Mario watched his departing figure. "I'm not sorry to see him go."

"Oh, Mario," Immaculata said soothingly, "don't pay attention to him. He's an angry person, and those kind are their own worst enemies. Let's go have a few dances before we turn in early. That is our plan, isn't it?" She batted her eyes at him.

"That's our plan. Let's go trip the light fantastic, baby." Mario smiled back at her as they pushed back their chairs. "Hope to see you all on deck early in the morning."

"We'll be there," Veronica said.

From across the room Milton appeared and offered his arm to Sylvie in a courteous but exaggerated way. "Shall we dance, my dear?"

Regan watched as Sylvie free-floated out of her chair. I wonder how he got rid of the sister, she thought. Regan was sure she'd appear out of nowhere before Milton and Sylvie finished their first hootchy-kootchy. Violet ought to apply for a job as a "Dating Game" chaperone. Either that or as a bouncer at a nightclub.

Dale put his napkin on the table. "Kenneth and I are off to the casino. See you later." He winked at Regan.

"We're going to see if we can finally win some money. We haven't had much luck so far, and this is our last chance," Kenneth added as they walked off.

Regan thought she saw Gabby twitch. "Are you turning in early tonight, Gavin?"

"I'm not sleepy," he insisted.

"Well, I must say I am," Veronica remarked. "This has been a delightful trip. All's well that ends well, right, Mr. Gray?"

"I hope so." Talk about last chances, he thought glumly.

Oxford

AT THE POLICE station Livingston ushered Val and Philip into his office. The transcripts of the Greek newspapers were on his desk. He opened them and handed the one with Val's picture to her.

"Is that you, Miss Twyler?"

Val nodded.

Livingston showed the picture to Philip. "I say, Val . . ." Philip's voice trailed off as though the absolute proof of Val's presence in the group picture with Athena had overwhelmed him.

"Professor, I'm going to ask you to wait in an adjoining room. I'd like to speak to Miss Twyler alone."

"Of course. Quite so." Philip got up heavily and walked slowly to the door. Livingston's assistant was waiting to escort him into a nearby office. Divide and conquer, the oldest police device of all, Livingston thought as he watched Philip's hunched shoulders and rumpled jacket fade from view.

Livingston noted that Philip had avoided Val's warning stare; it seemed a good sign that he did not make eye contact with her.

"Miss Twyler—a few questions."

She spent the next hour parrying with him, using exactly the reasoning he had expected from her. She had been the governess in the home of Athena's aunt when the terrible tragedy occurred. Naturally, like everyone else, she had been questioned. The police visited her repeatedly at the Pearsons Hall campus. You can imagine the gossip. She had no idea Athena had come to St. Polycarp's as a student.

"You never confided this to your fiancé, Professor Whitcomb?"

"There are some things we try to put behind us, not dig up."

"Like bodies?" Livingston suggested. "But obviously Philip confided something to you. What was it?"

"I don't know what he meant by that."

"You at one time had a blue Austin, isn't that right?"

"Yes." Her eyes narrowed.

"Do you happen to remember the license number?"

"No, I don't."

"Would it begin with three-one-five?"

"I don't remember."

"Miss Twyler, Athena Popolous had written 'B.A. three-one-five' on a matchbook cover from the Bull and Bear. Why do you suppose she did that?"

"I have no idea."

"Were you in the Bull and Bear on the night of April 23, 1982, when you came to Oxford for your interview?"

"I stopped to have a bite before I drove back to Pearsons Hall. I'm not sure which pub."

"Do you know a Cameron Hardwick?"

For the first time she looked flustered. "I'm not sure."

"The proprietor of the Barleyneck Inn can verify that you've rendezvoused there on and off for ten years."

"That was before I became engaged to Philip."

"You had tea in his room there last Saturday."

"To tell him I was getting married."

A cool one, Livingston thought again. "Isn't it quite a coincidence that Cameron Hardwick is on the *Queen Guinevere*?"

"No. He sails frequently."

"What does he do?"

"Investment counseling. There are many older women with a great deal of money on those cruises."

Possible, Livingston thought. Circumstantial, damn it, he fumed. Everything explainable. Every explanation possible. Tomorrow he'd talk to Regan in depth about Hardwick, and he'd also contact the NYPD; perhaps they had a file on him.

"May I please go home now, Inspector? I'm very tired."

Livingston looked at his watch. It was 2:05 A.M. "Let's wait a bit, shall we? I'd be happy to have someone fix you a cup of tea. And now I want to speak to Professor Whitcomb."

As he had hoped, Philip was a total wreck. Nervous. Terrified. Perspiring. Chewing on his fingernails. Whatever he has on his chest, he's dying to get rid of it, Livingston thought.

"Prof——Philip, if I may . . . There's something you want to tell me . . . something you've already confided to Miss Twyler. No innocent person has anything to worry about."

"Totally innocent . . . t-t-totally," Philip stammered.

Livingston made a stab in the dark. "Now sometimes any of us can be guilty of bad judgment," he suggested soothingly.

Bull's-eye. Philip gave one final bite to this thumbnail. "Bad judgment. Exactly. That's it. D-d-definitely should have called the authorities." He snapped his lips together.

"When?" Livingston whispered. "When, Philip?"

"Needed m-m-mulch, you see . . . n-n-never better than the stuff under the l-l-leaves in the woods. Compost heap and all that . . . breaks down to necessary ingredients . . . marvelous . . ."

"Yes, bad judgment, Philip, bad judgment," Livingston urged.

"You see, the year before Miss Po-Po-Popolous disappeared, terrible problem . . ."

"What was that?" Livingston felt as though he were trying to land a fish.

"An unstable young woman suggested that I impreg-preg-pregnated her. Impossible."

You won't have a hard time convincing me of that, Livingston thought.

"But quite unpleasant . . ." Philip gazed at the floor. "I had spent some time with h-h-her. Bad judgment . . ."

"Yes, Philip, yes . . ."

"And so the Saturday after Athena last showed up at class I was in the w-w-woods . . ."

"Yes . . ."

"You see, the poor dear girl used to bi-bi-bicycle past the house. It had been noted . . ."

"Yes . . ."

"I discovered her body!" Philip burst out.

"You discovered her body ten years ago!"

"T-t-terrible experience. Shovel hit it. Almost fainted, you know."

"And you didn't report it!"

"I was afraid because of what happened the y-y-year before . . . Didn't want to lose my job . . . was sure the body would be discovered by someone else . . ."

"And it never was?"

"N-n-no . . . until last week."

"You told Miss Twyler about this?"

"Yes . . . Had a little too much port one night . . . sort of blurted it out . . . Next day she suggested that if the b-b-body was ever found, it would be better if I was a m-m-married man."

That's one way to swindle a proposal, Livingston thought. "I see. I see."

"I really am quite content being alone with my flowers," Philip added forlornly.

At Sea

REGAN WATCHED VERONICA anxiously. Granted she'd been kicking up her heels for the past few days, but this sudden dramatic exhaustion was frightening. She had seemed progressively more tired toward the end of dinner, leaned on Regan as they left the elevator, barely seemed to have enough strength to shed the sequined cocktail dress.

Regan helped her into her nightgown and tucked her in. It's a good thing I talked her out of her bath, she thought. I'd have had to fish her out of the bubbles. She looked down at Veronica, already in a deep sleep, and felt a rush of compassion. She looks so vulnerable, especially since she hasn't started snoring yet, Regan thought guiltily.

Veronica's packing attempts had been a near disaster. Before dinner she had dumped the contents of all her bags in a frantic search for Sir Gilbert's poem on the joys of family life. She wanted to read it at the first meeting with her nieces.

Regan had found it in the pocket of the Sit-and-Be-Fit outfit Veronica had worn to the poetry session. "Of course, of course," Veronica cried happily. "I was planning to read this one second. 'Say, Say, Say' I committed to memory."

They'd barely had time to dress for dinner.

Now, with Veronica safely out of commission, Regan was able to begin the bewildering task of sorting out Veronica's clothes and repacking them. It took nearly two hours. It was midnight when Regan put the bags in the hall. She showered and climbed into the Castro. Bye, bye, Bernadette, she thought. Tomorrow night I'll be sleeping in a real bed.

She reached for the light, paused, got up and went to the door. She had locked it.

Regan turned the clock back an hour, as they'd been doing each night, and set the alarm for 3 A.M. The very prospect of getting up in less than four hours made her fall into an uneasy sleep.

MARIO AND IMMACULATA tiptoed down the corridor to the Merlin Suite. Immaculata giggled softly. "I feel like we're eloping," she whispered.

Mario fumbled with the key and dropped it. It made a faint *ping* as it bounced against the door. "Sssh," Immaculata said nervously. "If anyone finds out we're up here . . ."

By night the suite seemed even more glamorous than it had at cocktail hour. Mario dropped their overnight bags and reached for Immaculata. "Let me carry you over the threshold of the terrace," he offered grandly. "Oops."

"Mario, Mario, your back—I don't want you in traction."

"You're right." Mario rubbed his back. "I still have that tender spot."

"That's sciatica, Mario."

"Tell you what. I'll open the champagne. We'll drink it on the balcony."

Immaculata nodded. "I'll just slip inside and put on my new lingerie set."

A few minutes later, glasses in hand, Immaculata in her trailing black satin negligee and Mario in his boxer shorts and striped bathrobe toasted each other as the ship sped through the dark.

Oxford

LIVINGSTON FINISHED HIS fourth cup of tea. It was 4:30 A.M. in Oxford. "Now, Philip," he said kindly, "how do you suppose Miss Atwater got poisoned? Do you really think your aunt is capable of deliberately making anyone sick? Never mind risking an overdose!"

"N-no. No." Philip was slumped in his chair. His fingertips were raw. "If only I hadn't gone looking for that mulch."

"Now that you know Miss Twyler has not been honest with you, do you think your wedding plans will change?"

Philip nodded, his eyes hollow. "Quite a shock. I suppose it won't be possible to keep my finding of the body confidential."

Livingston shook his head. "I'm afraid not."

"I h-h-hope the headmaster will understand my predicament." Philip looked directly at Livingston. "No, I'm not going to marry Val."

"Isn't it true that what she basically did was blackmail you into an engagement and marriage?"

"She'd stop by the house . . . she could be very helpful. But I never, ever planned to marry her."

"Did you ever get the impression that if you did not marry her she might inadvertently let slip your little secret?"

"Well, if-if-if it ever slipped out, in-in-inadvertently, as she put it, she reminded me that a w-w-wife cannot be made to testify against her hu-hu-husband."

Livingston left him. In the hallway he growled to his assistant, "He's got all the worldliness of a two-year-old. The lady holds the answers here."

The assistant looked worried. "Sir, they're not charged and they are exhausted."

"And a young girl is dead, an elderly woman has been poisoned, and three children were left motherless. All when Valerie Twyler or Mary V. Cook was on the scene."

At Sea

AT 2 A.M. THE band played "After the Ball Is Over" and packed up their instruments. Gavin and Sylvie were sitting at the lounge bar.

"Some ball," Gavin muttered.

Sylvie looked at her old friend compassionately. "You look down in the dumps. What's the matter?"

"Nothing that a million bucks wouldn't cure." Gavin sipped his fourth vodka Collins. "You look pretty happy."

Sylvie hesitated, shrugged, leaned over and whispered in his ear. "Milton asked me to meet him at his home in Aspen next week, after he drops Violet off in Miami. He can't drop her hard enough for my money."

"Do you think this is the one—I mean the one you can land?"

"Don't be mean. I really think he's terrific."

"Don't sign any prenuptials."

At 2:15 A.M. Hardwick was ready. He had stopped at the casino, had a drink in the King's Lounge, then said a friendly good night to the bartender. His bags were in the hall.

He pulled on a hooded gray sweatshirt and matching jogging pants. He'd take the stairs instead of the elevator. They'd be deserted now. If he did bump into anyone, they'd assume he was a health nut on his way to the deck for a last run at sea.

It took less than a minute. He reached the penthouse floor and listened. The steward's station from which he'd stolen the key was around the bend in the corridor. There was no sign of life. The ten seconds he needed to get into the Exner suite and the ten to leave it and get back to the stairwell were his only vulnerable moments. Noiselessly he darted down the hall and slipped the key in the door of the Camelot Suite.

Nora Regan Reilly could not settle down. She moved, twisted, turned, plumped her pillow, sighed, sipped water from the glass on the night table. Beside her Luke was fast asleep.

Why was she so nervous? Ridiculous. She reminded herself that she always got antsy on the last night of a vacation. And it would be really fun to be with Regan. They were having brunch together at the Tavern on the Green in twelve hours. Only twelve hours more . . .

Oxford

IT HAD BEEN a long, long night. But Val at last was showing signs of unraveling. She kept glancing at her watch.

Why?

"Surely you don't have an appointment?" Livingston asked. "Most people don't get together before seven A.M."

In the last three hours he'd questioned Val about the felony murder in Greece. They had repeatedly gone over the fact that Val had tried to detain Helen Carvelous from going back to the house for her prescription sunglasses. That was why the Greek police had absolutely believed that Val had helped set up the burglary. Also, whoever broke into the home obviously knew the combination of the bedroom safe. And Val was always in and out of there with the children when Helen Carvelous dressed to go out. Helen Carvelous, who could never remember the combination of her safe, kept it written down in her dresser. Mary V. Cook knew that. "It still makes you an accessory to murder," Livingston reminded her. "Greek prisons are not attractive. You are now an accessory after the fact to Athena Popolous's death. The moment Philip told you about discovering the body, it was your duty as a citizen to report it."

She looked at her watch again. Beads of perspiration were forming on her forehead.

"Philip has told me he has no intention of marrying you. Frankly, I should think that wouldn't disturb you too much. From what I hear about Cameron Hardwick, he must be more your type."

"Philip and I are very much in love. Philip is understandably upset that I did not confide in him."

"Don't fool yourself, Miss Twyler. This will be nasty for Philip . . . could even cost him his job. But believe me, you'll never be mistress of Llewellyn Hall when Lady Exner dies. What is it, Miss Twyler?"

Val's face had gone chalk white. "She's going to die in a few minutes. And so is Regan Reilly."

At Sea

THE PHONE RANG. Groggily Regan opened her eyes and reached over, fumbling for the receiver. Fingers snapped around her wrist. A hand closed over her face. She felt her head being pushed down into the pillow. Electrified, she dug her teeth into the hand that was pressed against her mouth. With a muttered curse Hardwick loosened his grasp. Regan managed to scream once as the phone continued to ring.

"No answer there, sir." The ship's operator sounded sleepy. "They probably turned it off for the night."

"You must get through to them!"

"But they're not answering, sir. I could have a message slipped under the door," the sleepy voice droned.

Bloody nitwit, Livingston thought frantically. Waste of time trying to explain it to her. Regan's mother and father . . . better to get to them . . . What in hell was the father's name . . . ? "There's another Reilly on board. Put me through."

"We have two other Reillys, sir. Either Luke or—"

"Luke, that's it. PUT ME THROUGH!"

Immaculata's head was snuggled against Mario's barrel chest. He was contentedly sleeping. She was enjoying the luxury of the king-sized bed, storing in her memory every detail of the expensive suite and looking forward to the joyous reunion with Mario Jr. and the family, now only a few hours away.

She froze as she heard a faint but distinctive sound. Was that a scream? Was Lady Exner or that nice Regan having a nightmare? Careful not to awaken Mario, she slipped out of bed, tiptoed to the door, opened it a crack and listened. There was no further scream.

Someone was moving around in the other suite. Was Lady Exner sick? Maybe she should knock on the door and see if she could help. On the other hand, they were not supposed to be up here. Too uneasy to go back to bed, Immaculata stood indecisively, the door open a crack.

The phone rang. Like a shot Nora's arm grabbed the receiver. "Hello." She listened. "Oh my God," she shrieked. "Luke, Luke, someone's going to kill Regan!"

As Luke bolted from the bed, Nora sobbed, "Please, God, don't let us be too late."

Why doesn't Veronica wake up? She could call for help, Regan thought. She twisted to the side, frantically trying to escape her attacker. She tried to scream again. The sound was muffled as a pillow closed over her face. She kicked the blankets free. With all her strength she flailed her feet against him, catching him in the stomach. As he doubled over she got a faint glimpse of his face and recognized the man she had asked Livingston to investigate. Cameron Hardwick!

She rolled off the bed onto the carpet, sprang to her feet and started for the door. Her one advantage was her ability to move very quickly. The thought flashed across her mind that Veronica must have been drugged. Don't waste your breath screaming yet, she thought wildly. If she could get into the corridor . . .

Her hand was on the knob. She twisted it as an arm whipped around her waist, lifting her from the floor, a hand covered her mouth and she was pulled backward. An instant later the terrace door was sliding open. A cold blast of night wind hit her face. In her mind Regan could see the dark churning waters far below.

* * *

Gavin and Sylvie were just saying good night at the landing. He thought he was seeing an apparition. A barefooted Nora Regan Reilly, clad only in a clinging peach nightgown, sobbing wildly, was trying to keep up with her pajama-clad husband, who stopped uncertainly, realizing the staircase did not continue upward. Nora spotted Gavin.

"Gavin," Nora cried. "Regan, Lady Exner, how do we get to them?"

Luke grabbed his shoulders. "You've been there. Where are they?"

Gavin took in their distraught expressions and did not waste time with explanations. "Follow me!" he yelled.

Regan managed to grab the outside handle of the terrace door. She held on to it although her fingers felt as if they would break. The grip on her mouth was released. Hardwick was using that hand to try and pry her fingers loose. Now she was able to scream. It seemed to her that her anguished cry was carried away by the sound of the wind. Hardwick managed to break her grip on the handle. His hand rushed to cover her mouth. She threw her head to one side. He lost his balance on the slippery deck and they fell heavily together.

It was a scream, Immaculata thought, that definitely was a scream.

"Mario," she called urgently, "Mario, wake up."

In an instant, Mario was beside her. "What's the matter?"

She pointed to the Exner suite. "There's something wrong in there. That's the second time I heard someone scream. I'm sure of it."

At that moment footsteps pounded down the hall. Gavin Gray was running shoulder to shoulder with a man Mario had noticed in the restaurant. The man's wife and Sylvie were close behind them.

They stopped at the door of the Exner suite. Gavin twisted

the handle. "It's locked." Astounded, Mario watched as he and the other man threw their weight against the door.

Another faint scream. "Oh, dear God, that's Regan," Nora shrieked.

Mario shoved Gavin aside. "Get out of the way." The door splintered open as Mario threw his bull-like shoulder against it.

Mario and Luke stumbled together into the foyer. It was pitch-dark and cold inside the suite.

"Where the hell are the lights?" Luke demanded.

"Regan!" Nora screamed. "Regan, where are you?"

Gabby groped for the switches on the wall to the left of the doorframe. As he flipped them on, the suite and deck blazed into brightness.

The terrace door was open. Horrified, they saw Regan, her body arched over the railing, struggling to push away Cameron Hardwick. Her feet were flailing, her hair floating behind her as he relentlessly forced her backward.

Nora's scream was the bow, Luke's body the arrow. Racing across the sitting room, he dove through the doorway to the deck, butted Hardwick in the back, and as Regan fell managed to close his hand around her ankle when the rest of her body slid over the railing. Hardwick tackled him and they fell heavily to the deck as Luke frantically clawed at his daughter's foot, struggling to maintain his grip on it. Miraculously the weight was lifted.

"I've got her," Mario yelled. "I've got her." He dropped Regan to the safety of the deck, then fell next to Luke on the thrashing Cameron Hardwick.

"She's all right." Immaculata pressed a near-hysterical Nora to her ample bosom. "My Mario and the man in the maroon pajamas saved her."

Moans were coming from the king-sized bed. "I say, I say."

Sylvie rushed over to soothe Lady Exner. "The poor thing will have a heart attack."

Gavin, seeing that Regan was indeed all right, realized he had one last chance. He could always say he was getting a life preserver.

Forget the stool. He pushed over a chair and clambered up on it. Wildly he threw life preservers down. He reached for it. It was there. It was in his fingers. Thank you, Lord.

"Dear Mr. Gavin, what have you found?"

Lady Veronica Exner was fully awake.

KENNETH AND DALE came up the stairs, Kenneth with his beauty kit under one arm and a bottle of champagne under the other, as two grim-faced officers, each firmly holding the arms of a handcuffed Cameron Hardwick, emerged from the corridor that led to Lady Exner's suite.

Dale stopped. "What's going on?"

Hardwick ignored him.

Dale and Kenneth looked at each other. "Something's happened." They hurried down the hall, reached the open door of the suite and blinked in amazement. "Regan," Kenneth said, "you didn't tell us it was a pajama party. We would have brought more of the bubbly."

Lady Exner, a dazzling bracelet on her arm, chirped, "Mr. Gavin found Mrs. Watkins's bracelet. Isn't that lovely?"

Dale rushed to Sylvie. "He found the bracelet?"

Sylvie looked at Gavin with a sympathetic but knowing glance. "In a way he found it."

"But that's a fifty-thousand-dollar reward."

Gavin, who had been looking totally despondent, perked up. It might not be the Costa del Sol, but it was nothing to sneeze at.

Luke and Nora were standing by Regan as she talked on the phone to Superintendent Livingston. Now that the shock was over, Nora's natural whodunit curiosity had set in.

Regan was listening intently. When she started to say good-bye, Luke took the phone from her. "We can't thank you enough . . ."

Nora said to Regan, "What did he tell you?"

The room became suddenly still. Veronica seemed to have forgotten the bracelet. "Philip? Did he have anything to do with this?"

"Oh no, no. It was Val," Regan reassured her quickly. "Val and Cameron have been lovers off and on for years. He murdered Athena's aunt in Greece when she walked in on him during the robbery. They were both questioned in connection with the crime. The police were sure it was an inside job, and Val was the prime suspect.

"As Livingston said, you can imagine how shocked Athena must have been to see Val walk into a pub in Oxford and join Hardwick, who was wearing her uncle's priceless pocket watch that had been stolen with the other jewelry. According to Val's confession, Hardwick had pulled it out several times while he was waiting for her and they were afraid Athena might have seen it. Hardwick was sitting in a booth and hadn't noticed Athena was at the bar until Val came in and spotted her. Certainly it was obvious that Athena had put two and two together. Otherwise why would she have tried to jot down Val's license plate on the matchbook cover?"

Regan sighed. "They knew it would all be over if she went to the police. So they followed her out, caught up with her . . ."

"Why did she end up so near my property?" Veronica asked.

"Livingston thinks that Athena wanted to ask Philip what to do, and headed for Llewellyn Hall. She was emotionally dependent on him and had made him her unwilling confidant. Hardwick killed her near your house and they wanted to get rid of her body as fast as possible."

Regan hesitated. "Veronica, you must realize that Philip was totally unaware of Val's plans. She poisoned Penelope so that you'd be alone on this trip. Cameron Hardwick intended to make sure you didn't reach New York alive. With you dead and Val married to Philip, your estate would have been sold to that hotel chain in a minute. She couldn't take the chance that you might become close to your American relatives and change your will."

"But she was the one who suggested you come with me," Veronica protested.

"I had become a threat. She didn't know how much Athena might have told me about her aunt's death. She knew I was trying to recall everything. I keep a journal. I'm a trained investigator."

"I see." From her next question, it was clear that Veronica did see. "We met Val a year after the robbery in Greece. She always lived very modestly. What did she do with her share of all the valuable jewelry that was taken from the safe of Athena's aunt?"

Regan grinned. "Veronica, anytime you want a job in my office, you've got one. Hardwick was obsessed with that watch and took it as his share. It's priceless but would have been recognized immediately if he'd tried to sell it. He's always kept it. Val sold the stones from her share of the jewelry for two hundred thousand dollars and put the money in a safe deposit box. Her finances have been under intense police scrutiny all these years and she knew it. She made what she considered a good bargain with her sometime lover. He would get rid of us. As Philip's wife she could live in the style she wanted as soon as the Llewellyn Hall property was sold. And Hardwick would have the watch and get two hundred thousand dollars in cash."

Veronica nodded. "I see. I see. Perhaps I shouldn't have kept my wonderful news till next year."

"News?" Regan asked.

"Of course I'm going to leave Llewellyn Hall, the fifty acres immediately surrounding it, and a trust to Philip. The rest I'm giving to Saint Polycarp's, to be used to set up the Sir Gilbert Exner Poetry Center. Dear Philip will continue to extend his magic with the flowers. And it goes without saying that he will have a lifetime professorship at Saint Polycarp's."

"That's wonderful, Veronica," Regan said as she wondered how the relatives waiting on the pier would react to this news.

Everyone stayed in the Camelot Suite, drank champagne and cheered the Statue of Liberty when they sailed into the harbor.

Luke and Nora invited one and all to join them at the Tavern on the Green for brunch.

"Do they allow children?" Immaculata asked hopefully.

"Sure they do," Luke said heartily.

Sylvie asked anxiously, "Can you put up with Violet? Her plane to Florida doesn't leave until five."

"She was the first one to tie Cameron Hardwick to Greece. Believe me, she's welcome," Regan said.

Dale turned to Kenneth. "Let's change our flight home and stay until tomorrow."

"Done."

The thought of the fifty-thousand-dollar check and no nightmares about the cops ever catching up with him had transformed Gavin into a near-euphoric mood. He'd spend the rest of the day on the phone talking to all the columnists. Who knows? Maybe he'd get "Gavin's Guests" back on the air.

New York

THEY GOT THROUGH customs in a mercifully short time. The only near catastrophe was when Veronica went to pet one of the drug-sniffing German shepherds. "Precious, precious," she murmured as Regan yanked her hand back.

There was no mistaking the Buttacavola clan, Regan thought affectionately. They were standing directly in front of the customs gate. Mario Junior was a carbon copy of his father. Regan had seen so many pictures of Roz, Mario the Third and Concepcione that she could have picked them out of an aerial shot of Yankee Stadium.

Immaculata swooped down on the children, crushing the bouquet of roses Mario the Third was attempting to hand her. "Wait till we tell you what a hero your grandpa is," she cried as she smothered them with kisses.

"Mommy just threw up," Mario the Third reported as he struggled free from his grandmother's clutches.

"Roz, are you all right?" Immaculata asked in an alarmed voice.

"Morning sickness, Grandma," Roz bragged with an ear-to-ear smile. "Nunzio or Fortunata will arrive in time for Valentine's Day."

"AAAAAHHHHHH!" Immaculata's scream of delight drowned out the sound of traffic on the West Side Highway.

It was also easy to pick out Veronica's cousin and her two daughters. The mother was holding a sign. WELCOME, AUNT VERONICA.

"Ah, there they are, my flesh and blood," Veronica cried as she ran to them. They all dropped into a curtsy.

It won't do you any good, pals, Regan thought.

* * *

"Hey, Regan. Regan." Jeff's familiar voice made her spin around. A moment later he was sweeping her up. Over his shoulder she could see Kit's smiling face.

"I brought you some chocolates," Jeff said. "Somebody in first class gave them to me."

"Thanks a lot! The last guy who gave me chocolates tried to bill me." It was great to see the two of them.

Kit was waving a letter. "The first request for donations to Saint Polycarp's arrived by Express Mail!"

They all clinked glasses at Tavern on the Green.

"My God, those kids can eat," Kit muttered in a low voice.

Violet Cohn, thoroughly pleased to have been right, was telling Kenneth and Dale how impossibly rude Cameron had been when he waited on them in Greece. "Can you believe I overheard him calling me an old bag?" Their looks of profound shock would have done credit to Sir Laurence Olivier.

Regan could tell that Sylvie and Milton were holding hands under the table.

Gavin was devoting himself to Nora. "When I get 'Gavin's Guests' back on the air, I want you to be on the first program. Boy, will we have a lot to tell the audience."

Luke murmured, "Nora, be sure to set the dial before you leave the house."

Veronica turned her attention from her adoring relatives. "And I want a tape of it sent to me. Nora is so dear. Regan told me that the two of you didn't want me worrying about working on my life story while we were on the ship. That's so thoughtful. Well, now we have a chance to spend time together." She raised her glass. "To a wonderful month with my relatives and friends and a safe and exciting cruise home. Regan, do you think you'd like to see me back?"

Regan gasped. "Well, I-I-I don't know, Veronica." My God, she thought, I'm starting to sound like Philip. "Superintendent Livingston tells me that Penelope is dying to join you in New York. Maybe you should give her a chance."

"You're right, Regan. The poor dear has had a dreadful time because of me . . ."

"Just one thing," Regan added. "Warn her to leave her recipe for tasty pasties home. They'd never allow it through customs."